AF576886

THE GRAYWOLF ANNUAL TWO

SHORT STORIES BY WOMEN

EDITED BY SCOTT WALKER

GRAYWOLF PRESS : SAINT PAUL

The stories collected in this *Graywolf Annual* appeared previously in publications, as noted below. We gratefully acknowledge the cooperation of editors, agents and the authors.

Susan Minot's "The Navigator" was first published in *Grand Street*. Reprinted by permission of Georges Borchardt, Inc., and the author. Copyright © 1985 by Susan Minot.

Louise Erdrich's "The Beet Queen" appeared in *The Paris Review*. Copyright © 1985 by Louise Erdrich.

Alice Munro's "Walker Brothers Cowboy" was published in *The Literary Review* in 1985. It is part of her early collection *Dance of the Happy Shades*, republished in 1985 by Penguin Books. Copyright © 1968 by Alice Munro.

Joy Williams's "Health" was first published in *Tendril*. Copyright © 1985 by Joy Williams.

Alice Adams's "The Oasis" was published and syndicated by Fiction Network. Copyright © 1985 by Alice Adams.

Jane Bowles's "Señorita Córdoba" was published in *The Threepenny Review*. Copyright © 1985 by Paul Bowles for the Estate of Jane Bowles.

Laurie Colwin's "Old Flames" was published in *The New Yorker*. Reprinted by permission of Candida Donadio and Associates, Inc. Copyright © 1985 by Laurie Colwin.

Ann Beattie's "Cards" first appeared in *Esquire*. Copyright © 1985 by Ann Beattie.

Elizabeth Tallent's "Black Holes" was published in *The New Yorker*. Copyright © 1985 by Elizabeth Tallent.

Sara Vogan's "Sunday's No Name Band" was selected for inclusion in the PEN/NEA. Syndicated Fiction Project. Copyright © 1984 by Sara Vogan.

Bobbie Ann Mason's "Blue Country" was published and syndicated by Fiction Network. Copyright © 1985 by Bobbie Ann Mason.

Tess Gallagher's "Bad Company" first appeared in *Ploughshares*. Copyright © 1985 by Tess Gallagher.

Mavis Gallant's "Irina" is from *From the Fifteenth District*, published by Random House, Inc. Reprinted by permission of Georges Borchardt, Inc., and the author. Copyright © 1985 by Mavis Gallant.

Publication of this volume is made possible in part by a grant from the National Endowment for the Arts, and in part by generous contributions to Graywolf Press from individuals, corporations and foundations.

ISBN 0-915308-78-9 / ISSN 0743-7471
Library of Congress Catalog Card Number 85-80978
First printing, 1986
Designed by Tree Swenson
Joanna type set by Walker & Swenson

Published by Graywolf Press, Post Office Box 75006, Saint Paul, Minnesota 55175.

THE GRAYWOLF SHORT FICTION SERIES

TABLE OF CONTENTS

THE GRAYWOLF ANNUAL TWO

SHORT STORIES BY WOMEN

SUSAN MINOT

The Navigator

IN THE SUMMER they ate early, everyone drifting home like particles in a tide. By evening most of the people had disappeared from the wharf and the North Eden harbor was quiet, the thoroughfare running by as flat as a slab of granite. Tonight there was a fog coming in. It was the end of August and all seven of the Vincent children – four girls and three boys – were up there in Maine.

Gus came in off the dock. The screen door ticked out its long yawn and when he reached the kitchen at the end of the short hall it clapped shut.

The girls were making dinner. Delilah shook salt into the pots on the stove; Sidney peeled a cucumber.

Gus propped his foot against the icebox and bumped against the door frame.

"Work hard?" Sidney said.

Gus nodded. He had been housepainting all summer; his dark skin was specked with white.

Sidney ran a fork down the side of the cucumber and held it up next to Gus's face. "For your skin," she said. He closed his eyes to feel the spray.

Delilah folded her arms. "It's just us tonight," she said. "Mum and Dad are going to the Irvings'."

"Dad is?" Gus said. "What is it, skit night?"

"Practically," Sidney said. She picked up a cigarette from the ashtray, took a drag and gave it to Gus. "They're playing Find the Button."

Gus smiled. "Which one's that?"

"You know. They hide the things – a thimble on the lampshade or a golf tee in the peanuts – the button camouflaged in some flowers. When you spot it, you write it down."

"How'd Mum get him to go?" Gus rubbed the ash into his pants. The bottoms were rolled up in doughnuts.

"God knows," said Sidney.

"It was a choice between that and the Kittredges' clambake on Friday," Delilah said.

They all laughed.

Delilah was crumbling hamburger. "Poor guy," she said to the frying pan.

"He can handle it," Sidney said.

Gus left them and went into the living room. Chicky, the youngest of the boys, was sitting on the creaking wicker sofa. Going by, Gus swatted the back of his head. On the record player, Bob Dylan was singing "Tangled Up in Blue" for the millionth time. Certain records stayed in North Eden all year long – they were the rejects, hopelessly warped. Still, they got put on again and again. Hearing those songs straight through somewhere else was always a surprise.

Gus took his book off the pile of *National Geographic* and *Harvard* magazines. He stretched out on the window seat, opened the book and set it face down on his stomach.

"Went to the quarry," Chicky said. He was whittling at a stick with his Swiss Army knife. "The bottomless one."

"Right," Gus said. He smiled out the window at the floats. The Jewel girls were down there climbing out of their stinkpot. A light mist drifted by in thin trails.

"It was," Chicky said. Shavings littered the floor by his bare feet.

"Chicky, it's impossible," his older brother said. "Quarries're man-made."

Chicky worked over a little knot. "You can think what you want," he said.

From the kitchen, Sidney called, "Where's Minna?" The boys didn't answer. The screen door slammed. "I'm right here," came the seven-year-old voice from the hall. Sidney and little Miranda came into the living room at the same time from separate doors.

Sidney said, "Will someone go tell Ma?"

"Is it supper?" Gus asked.

"Five minutes."

"Good," Chicky said.

"Who's going to tell Ma?" Sidney said, holding a stack of napkins at her throat.

Minnie climbed onto Gus's lap and perched on her shins. Gus said, "Minnie will, won't she, Minniana?"

"Do I have to?"

"I would but we're getting supper," Sidney said. She stepped into the dining room but stayed within earshot.

"I always do," said Minnie, collapsing on her brother.

Caitlin walked in. "You always do what?" she asked. Her hair was wet and she hit at it from underneath to dry. She was the oldest.

"Well, somebody better go," Sidney said from the dining room. Her head appeared. "Gus, will you?"

Gus winced.

"What?" Caitlin said.

"Why don't you ask Sherman?" Chicky said. He pointed out the window. "He never goes."

Sherman, the middle brother, was standing outside at the dock railing. He was spitting over the edge and watching it land in the water. Someone must have tapped on the window above him – Mum and Dad were upstairs getting dressed – because Sherman turned and looked up. His eyes revealed nothing, like Indian eyes.

"Sure," Sidney said. "Good luck."

Minnie kept her head against Gus's chest. "*He's* not about to get Ma," she said.

"Why not?" Caitlin said. She huffed over to the window and lifted it. A damp mist came rolling over the sill. "Sherman," she said, her voice sounding cottony outside. "Go tell Ma it's supper."

Sherman turned his head. "Why don't you?" he said.

"Because I'm asking you to."

Sherman glanced past her. "Why doesn't Chicky go?" he said.

"I don't believe this," Sidney said.

Chicky's knife peeled a long curl. "She'll come over anyway," he said.

Caitlin turned around to him with her mouth set.

Delilah stood in the doorway with a potholder mitten on. "Has someone gone to get Ma?"

"Gee, Deliliah," Gus said. "We thought you'd gone."

"This is ridiculous," Caitlin said. "Come on, Minnie. Go."

Minnie's little back went stiff. "I always do." She shifted off Gus.

"It's not going to kill you," Caitlin said.

Minnie trudged out of the room. They heard the screen door swing, then slam. From where he sat, Gus could see her padding over on the dock to Ma's house. He made a moping face and rocked from side to side, imitating her.

The girls laughed.

THE DINING ROOM had cream-colored walls and two windows that faced the harbor. At high tide, the water rose right up to the shingles and the light made criss-crossing patterns on the low ceiling. It was a small room, just fitting the long table.

Ma, who was Dad's mother, lived by herself in the far house. Her cook, Livia, had gone back to Ireland so that kitchen was no longer used. Before supper, Ma read in her living room and had her glasses of sherry. By the time she got to the other house for dinner with her grandchildren, her face was always flushed.

She sat down, wobbling, at her usual place.

Delilah had a plate at the side table. "Sherman, can you wait? I'm getting this for Ma."

Ma had on a smile. She smiled at the children, smiled at the candle flame, smiled at the blue bowl of grated cheese. "Isn't this nice," she said, smiling. Four small vases of nasturtiums from the garden were on the table.

Gus stood at the window, holding his plate over his chest. "Foggy," he said.

"Is it?" Sidney said. She was busy with wooden spoons in the salad. Everyone bustled around. Caitlin poured milk for Minnie.

Gus nodded and touched his forehead to the pane. "Everything's disappearing," he said.

They'd been eating for a while when Dad came in. He rubbed his hands together. "Evening, evening," he said, shifting from one foot to the other.

"You look pretty snappy," Sidney said. He was wearing a yellow blazer and his tie with the green anchors on it. His face looked freshly slapped.

"Mum assures me I won't be allowed in Lally Irving's house without the proper attire," he said, bent slightly at the waist.

"You look great," Caitlin said.

Dad smiled dismissively.

Mum came in smelling of perfume, wearing a long skirt. "See you later, Monkeys," she said. She plucked a carrot stick from the salad.

Ma beamed at Mum. "Rosie," she said.

Mum's real name was Rose Marie – it was Irish – but she'd changed it, thanks to Dad. He called her Rosie after the schoolteacher in *The African Queen* who dumps out all of Humphrey Bogart's whiskey in order to get them down the river. Mum never drank at all.

She looked at her family in the candlelight. "Okey-dokey," she said.

"Good luck finding the button," Gus said.

"Who needs luck?" Mum said, kicking out her foot. "You're looking at last year's champ. Come on, Uncs, off we go." Her nickname for Dad was Uncle.

Dad bowed, putting his palms together, and followed after her. Everyone at the table chuckled. Ma was smiling. She held her fork over her plate but still had not touched her food.

EARLY THE NEXT MORNING Gus woke up the boys to explain what had happened.

"They got home from the Irvings'," Gus said, "and Mum couldn't get him down the steps."

There were five flights of granite which led down from the street. Gus and the girls had heard Mum call "Yoo hoo." Gus went up the steps to help Dad down. The girls stood in the floodlight of the underpass, watching in the fog. Gus and Mum brought him into the light. Collapsed between them, Dad had been smiling grandly. He caught sight of his daughters in a semicircle and beamed toward them. Receiving no response, he had made a *whoops* expression and covered his mouth, giggling.

Gus sat on Sherman's bed but faced Chicky. "We're going to talk to him this morning," he said.

"What for," Sherman said. "Let the guy do what he wants."

The girls were downstairs with Mum, except for Minnie, who was at sailing class.

"He didn't want to go in the first place," Mum said, washing dishes at the sink. "I shouldn't have made him."

Caitlin waited by the toaster. "What happened?" she asked.

"He was okay till dinner," Mum said. She gazed through the window in front of her; the shingles of the house next door were a foot away. "Then half-way through the roast beef he decided he was finished and plopped his plate down on top of Mrs. Aberdeen's."

They all smiled in spite of themselves.

"What did Mrs. Aberdeen do?" Delilah said.

Mum shook her head.

Caitlin was serious. "Then what?"

"He collapsed on his placemat with his hands over his head." Mum turned to her daughters. "He said, 'This is so *boring*.'"

Caitlin was still. "You're kidding."

"Then – " Mum took a breath. "Everyone pretended it was

time to go and they put their jackets back on and we all said good-bye and they helped Dad find his way to the car. After we drove off, I imagine they went back in and finished dinner."

Sidney said, "You mean they faked going home?"

Mom shrugged: that was nothing.

The boys were shuffling in. Mum said, "He won't listen to me. I'm like a buzz in his ear."

They waited at the table, the girls at the near end, the boys next to the windows.

Sidney heard Dad and set down her knife. Delilah straightened in her chair. Dad came in with his plate and put it down. Caitlin bit delicately into her muffin, stealing glances in Dad's direction. Dad went back into the kitchen and returned with a carton of orange juice. He poured a glass and drank it standing up.

Mum was beside him, holding the back of her chair. Her scarf was rolled into a hairband above her wide forehead. She had on a lavender turtleneck.

"The kids want to talk to you, Uncs," she said and slipped into her seat.

Dad pulled out his chair noisily. He buttered his toast, not waiting for the butter to melt. "You ready for a little golf today, Sherman?" he said, not looking up.

Gus looked at Sherman, then at his father, then at Mum. Mum was pressing crumbs with her fingers and brushing them off, making a little pile. Chicky was interested in something under the table. He made a noise to call the cat. Sherman sat heavily, no breakfast plate in front of him, his hands in his lap.

Caitlin spoke first. "Do you remember last night?"

Dad's chin traced out a long nod.

"How's your arm?" Delilah asked.

"My hand," he said and held it up. "Stiff." He put it back down and, with his good hand, folded some toast around his bacon and took a bite.

Half-way down the steps, he had broken free of Gus and Mum and keeled over into the unguarded rubble. There had been a trickling of small stones after him. The girls watched helplessly as he got onto his hands and knees. His head had wobbled like one of those toy dogs people have on their dashboards. The girls looked away.

"Dad, do you remember talking to me?" Gus said.

"Yes," said his father, addressing the jar of beach-plum jelly in front of him.

"What?" Delilah said.

Dad's frown was like a twitch. "Yes," he repeated.

"Do you remember what you said you'd do?" Gus asked.

Dad dipped his rolled-up toast into his mug of coffee. He nodded.

"Well?" Caitlin said. "What about it?"

Dad chewed, keeping his mouth closed. He looked around the table with an innocent expression.

Sidney said, "We have to talk about it."

"Fine," he said.

While Gus was bringing him upstairs, the girls had lingered in the hall with Mum. Above them, they heard Gus's urgent voice. They sat on the bottom step, transfixed. His voice was pleading, "We all do...because whenever we try...can't stand it when you..."

Outside some footsteps had banged by – two figures in yellow slickers passed the doorway – their steps ringing woodenly on the dock. But the girls hardly noticed, glancing over like sleep-walkers. The fog blew by through the underpass.

Above them they had heard Dad say, "Imagine that."

Caitlin covered her knuckles and slouched forward on the table. "So will you stop?" She looked at Mum. Mum was gazing out the window.

Dad looked at Caitlin as if she were speaking another language.

Sidney said, "You have to, Dad," and her voice wavered. Dad turned to her with the same face, blank but suspecting insult.

"Well?" Caitlin said.

Chicky pointed toward the water. "Look," he said.

Everyone turned. A huge green cattle boat had entered the window frame, undulating behind the tiny streaks in the glass.

The white sails were as flat as building sides. It changed the light in the dining room.

"Looks like the *Horn of Plenty,*" Mum said brightly.

Everyone watched it glide into the second window.

"No," Sherman said. It was a mystery how he knew these things. "That's *Captain's Folly.*"

When Dad was young he had worked summers on a cattle boat that cruised through the islands. He'd been the navigator. He still had an astronomy book on the bottom shelf of his bed-side table.

"Is it anchoring?" Sidney said.

Delilah shook her head. "It's just passing through."

The sailboat slipped out of the window frame. Gus tipped back his chair to keep it in sight. It continued through the thoroughfare. At the outer cove, its sails buckled and a tiny figure at the bow lowered a huge anchor into the water. Gus set his chair down and faced back in.

Dad hit the table with his hand like a gavel and started to get up.

"Wait," Caitlin said. "Dad." His frown was attentive. She ducked and went on, "We think you need help."

Dad glanced at Mum. She was fiddling with her pearl earring. Her other hand came up for an adjustment.

"You do, Dad," Sidney said.

Dad's gaze went over the table – the green vases of red nasturtiums, some Sugar Pops casting pebble shadows.... He reached into his pocket, hitching up his whole side as if mounting a horse. "Okay," he said uncertainly. He brought out a pack of cigarettes and stirred his finger in the opening. When he lit one, it burned half-way down in the first drag.

Sidney covered her forehead. "Okay what?" she said.

Dad looked at her with a cold eye. Delilah nudged her; she kept facing Dad. His posture was stiff and erect and his lips were pressed smartly together.

Caitlin lifted her chin toward him. "Okay what?" she said.

His eyes glared. She shrank back. As he put out his cigarette, his throat seemed to swell, as if his Adam's apple were expanding and the whole of his uncomfortable being were struggling there in his throat. He coughed. "I won't drink," he said.

Was that it? Caitlin began to smile. Sidney picked up a muffin crust and tapped it on her plate.

Gus said, "But, Dad, do you think – ?"

"I said, 'I won't drink.'"

"I know, but..." Gus inspected his hands lying flat in front of him.

Delilah said, "That's great, Dad."

Dad's chair scraped the floor and he stood up. Mum had a satisfied face. "Okay, Monkeys," she said, "where shall we take the picnic?"

THE SKY WAS smooth blue and clear. Ma watched from her balcony while they streamed out to the boat. A book lay in her lap. She had stopped going on picnics. Each one said good-bye to her, passing beneath her with their towels and books and baskets. Ma held a cigarette pinched elegantly between thumb and finger. The skirt of her print dress stirred against the chair.

Random River was at the end of one of the coves that scalloped off the thoroughfare. A tidal river, it was a muddy bed dotted with boulders at low tide. When the tide was high a boat could motor up there. Even then rocks appeared, just breaking the surface.

Dad stood at the wheel of the fiberglass motorboat. His seven children were arranged in various perches; the motor gurgled at a slow speed. Mum sat beside him behind the windshield with her round sunglasses on. Usually there was much advice about the rocks, or Dad would appoint a lookout. "You're heading right for one!" "No no! To the left!" Today, there wasn't a peep. Dad navigated his way down the swirling turns, over the dimpled water.

It was glassy along the shore, the water dark green and shaded, bugs leaving pinpricks here and there. Bristling out of the rocks was the stiff grass – a porous leaf that slashed your calves when you were wading. There were tiny slugs clinging to the blades.

The Vincents glided toward their rock. They always went to the same rock. It had a plateau where the picnic basket got put and a scooped-out place where you could lie in the sun. In the photo albums there were lots of pictures taken here.

Gus stepped over the bow railing and crouched at the front.

"Careful," Mum said.

He leapt onto the rock and turned to fend off the bow.

"Eggshell landing," Caitlin said.

They all felt the crunch. "Whoops," Sidney said. But nothing was going to disturb the dreamy contentment that had taken over.

They unloaded, balancing cushions and coolers, lowering Minnie by her armpits. Delilah gripped Mum's arm while she stepped down. At the stern, Dad flung the anchor into the water. Gus led the painter into a jumble of rocks.

The sun streaked across the long ripples of the lagoon. Had Ma been there, she'd have already been in. Sidney tested the water. Everyone moved about politely. Caitlin squinted into the sun, then lay out her towel. She tugged the towel over to make room for Sidney. Mum pulled Minnie's sweatshirt over her head and her pigtails popped out.

"Listen to this," Delilah said. She had a magazine across her thighs. " 'The two hundred couples exchanged vows beneath a grape bower on the Reverend's California estate.' "

"Sick," Mum said. She settled her head back on Minnie's life jacket.

" 'Afterwards, the wedded devotees reaffirmed their faith in a baptismal ceremony in the garden fountains.' "

"Unbelievable," Caitlin said.

Sherman was rummaging around in the picnic basket. He stood up with a handful of Fritos and crunched them one at a time. Dad carried the cooler up higher into the shade. There was a toppled tree up there, with roots that spread in a fan. When they were younger, the kids used to stand in front of it and hoot and listen for the echo. It was like a half-shell, the way the sounds reverberated. Up close, the roots and moss made intricate designs, like an ancient chart. Chicky was digging at a groove in the rock with a stick, idly but persistently. Gus and Minnie squatted over some curly black lichen. "Indian corn flakes," Gus said. Minnie laughed. It was quiet and pleasant and there was no noise except the drone of a motorboat somewhere out on the water.

Then they all heard the sound.

They sometimes heard noises far off – a *crack* like that – someone with a shotgun who knew what he was doing, or a pickup backfiring on the South Eden bridge farther down the river. But none of the picnickers mistook this sound.

Some heads jerked toward Dad; some looked down. Above them, Dad was facing the root screen, his back to the family. Mum didn't move, lying on the life jacket, eyes hidden behind her sunglasses. Sidney hugged her shins and bit her knee. Gus's neck was twisted into a tortured position; he glared at Dad's back.

Dad turned around. He gazed with an innocent expression out over the snaking water. If aware of the eyes upon him, Dad did not betray it, observing the scenery with contentment; nothing more normal than for him to be standing in the shade at a family picnic holding a can of beer. He twisted the ring from its opening and, squinting at a far-off view, stooped to lap up the nipple of foam at the top of the can.

The silence was no longer tranquil.

Sometimes on still black nights they had had throwing contests off the dock. They threw stones into the thoroughfare and listened to hear them land. Sometimes the darkness would swallow up a stone and they'd wait, but no sound would come. It seemed then as if the stone had gone into some further darkness, entered some other dimension where things went on falling and falling.

LOUISE ERDRICH

The Beet Queen

LONG BEFORE they planted beets in Argus and built the highways, there was a railroad. Along the track, which crossed the Dakota-Minnesota border and stretched on east to Minneapolis, everything that made the town arrived. All that diminished the town departed by that route too. On a cold spring morning in 1932 the train brought both an addition and a subtraction. They came by freight. By the time they reached Argus their lips were violet and their feet were so numb that, when they jumped out of the boxcar, they stumbled and scraped their palms and knees through the cinders.

The boy was a tall fourteen, hunched with his sudden growth and very pale. His mouth was sweetly curved, his skin fine and girlish. His sister was only eleven years old, but already she was so short and ordinary that it was obvious she would be this way all her life. Her name was as square and practical as the rest of her: Mary. She brushed her coat off and stood in the watery wind. Between the buildings there was only more bare horizon for her to see, and from time to time men crossing it. Wheat was the big crop then, and this topsoil was so newly tilled that it hadn't all blown off yet, the way it had in Kansas. In fact, times were generally much better in eastern North Dakota than in most places, which is why Karl and Mary Lavelle had come there on the train. Their mother's sister, Fritzie, lived on the eastern edge of town. She ran a butcher shop with her husband.

The two Lavelles put their hands up their sleeves and started walking. Once they began to move they felt warmer although they'd been traveling all night and the chill had reached in deep. They walked east, down the dirt and planking of the broad main street, reading the signs on each false-front clapboard store they passed, even reading the gilt letters in the window of the brick bank. None of these places was a butcher shop. Abruptly, the stores stopped and a string of houses, weathered gray or peeling gray, with dogs tied to their porch railings, began.

Small trees were planted in the yards of a few of these houses and one tree, weak, a scratch of light against the gray of everything else, tossed in a film of blossoms. Mary trudged solidly forward, hardly glancing at it, but Karl stopped. The tree drew him with its delicate perfume. His cheeks were pink, he stretched his arms out like a sleepwalker, and in one long transfixed motion he floated to the tree and buried his face in the white petals.

Turning to look for Karl, Mary was frightened by how far back he had fallen and how still he was, his face pressed in the flowers. She shouted, but he did not seem to hear her and only stood, strange and stock-still, among the branches. He did not move even when the dog in the yard lunged against its rope and bawled. He did not notice when the door to the house opened and a woman scrambled out. She shouted at Karl too, but he paid her no mind and so she untied her dog. Large and anxious, it flew forward in great bounds. And then, either to protect himself or to seize the blooms, Karl reached out and tore a branch from the tree.

It was such a large branch, from such a small tree, that blight would attack the scar where it was pulled off. The leaves would fall away later that summer and the sap would sink into the roots. The next spring, when Mary passed it on some errand, she saw that it bore no blossoms and remembered how, when the dog jumped for Karl, he struck out with the branch and the petals dropped around the dog's fierce outstretched body in a sudden snow. Then he yelled, "Run!" and Mary ran east, toward Aunt

Fritzie. But Karl ran back to the boxcar and the train.

SO THAT'S HOW I came to Argus. I was the girl in the stiff coat. After I ran blind and came to a halt, shocked not to find Karl behind me, I looked up to watch for him and heard the train whistle long and shrill. That was when I realized Karl had jumped back on the same boxcar and was now hunched in straw, watching out the opened door. The only difference would be the fragrant stick blooming in his hand. I saw the train pulled like a string of black beads over the horizon, as I have seen it so many times since. When it was out of sight, I stared down at my feet. I was afraid. It was not that with Karl gone I had no one to protect me, but just the opposite. With no one to protect and look out for, I was weak. Karl was taller than me but spindly, older of course, but fearful. He suffered from fevers that kept him in a stuporous dream state and was sensitive to loud sounds, harsh lights. My mother called him delicate, but I was the opposite. I was the one who begged rotten apples from the grocery store and stole whey from the back stoop of the creamery in Minneapolis, where we were living the winter after my father died.

This story starts then, because before that and without the year 1929, our family would probably have gone on living comfortably and even have prospered on the Minnesota land that Theodor Lavelle broke and plowed and where he brought his bride, Adelaide, to live. But because that farm was lost, bankrupt like so many around it, our family was scattered to chance. After the foreclosure, my father worked as day labor on other farms in Minnesota. I don't even remember where we were living the day that word came. I only remember that my mother's hair was plaited in two red crooked braids and that she fell, full length, across the floor at the news. It was a common grain-loading accident, and Theodor Lavelle had smothered in oats. After that we moved to a rooming house in the Cities, where my mother thought that, with her figure and good looks, she could find work in a fashionable store. She didn't know, when we moved, that she was pregnant. In a surprisingly short amount of time we were desperate.

I didn't know how badly off we were until my mother stole six heavy, elaborately molded silver spoons from our landlady, who was kind or at least harbored no grudge against us, and whom my mother counted as a friend. Adelaide gave no explanation for the spoons, but she probably did not know I had discovered them in her pocket. Days later, they were gone and Karl and I owned thick overcoats. Also, our shelf was loaded with green bananas. For several weeks we drank quarts of buttermilk and ate buttered toast with thick jam. It was not long after that, I believe, that the baby was ready to be born.

One afternoon my mother sent us downstairs to the landlady. This woman was stout and so dull that I've forgotten her name although I recall vivid details of all else that happened at that time. It was a cold late-winter afternoon. We stared into the glass-faced cabinet where the silver stirrup cups and painted plates were locked after the theft. The outlines of our faces stared back at us like ghosts. From time to time Karl and I heard someone groan upstairs. It was our mother, of course, but we never let on as much. Once something heavy hit the floor directly above our heads. Both of us looked up at the ceiling and threw out our arms involuntarily, as if to catch it. I don't know what went through Karl's mind, but I thought it was the baby, born heavy as lead, dropping straight through the clouds and my mother's body. Because Adelaide insisted that the child would come from heaven although it was obviously growing inside of her, I had a confused idea of the process of birth. At any rate, no explanation I could dream up accounted for the groans, or for the long scream that tore through the air, turned Karl's face white, and caused him to slump forward in the chair.

I had given up on reviving Karl each time he fainted. By that time I trusted that he'd come to by himself, and he always did, looking soft and dazed and somehow refreshed. The most I ever did was support his head until his eyes blinked open. "It's born," he said when he came around, "let's go upstairs."

But as if I knew already that our disaster had been accomplished in that cry, I would not budge. Karl argued and made a case for at least going up the stairs, if not through the actual door, but I sat firm and he had all but given up when the landlady came back downstairs and told us, first, that we now had a baby brother, and, second, that she had found one of her grandmother's silver spoons under the mattress and that she wasn't going to ask how it got there, but would only say we had two weeks to get out.

The woman probably had a good enough heart. She fed us before she sent us upstairs. I suppose she wasn't rich herself, could not be bothered with our problems, and besides that, she felt betrayed by Adelaide. Still, I blame the landlady in some measure for what my mother said that night, in her sleep.

I was sitting in a chair beside Adelaide's bed, in lamp light, holding the baby in a light wool blanket. Karl was curled in a spidery ball at Adelaide's feet. She was sleeping hard, her hair spread wild and bright across the pillows. Her face was sallow and ancient with what she had been through, but after she spoke I had no pity.

"We should let it die," she mumbled. Her lips were pale, frozen in a dream. I would have shaken her awake but the baby was nestled hard against me.

She quieted momentarily, then she turned on her side and gave me a long earnest look.

"We could bury it out back in the lot," she whispered, "that weedy place."

"Mama, wake up," I urged, but she kept speaking.

"I won't have any milk. I'm too thin."

I stopped listening. I looked down at the baby. His face was round, bruised blue, and his eyelids were swollen almost shut. He looked frail, but when he stirred I put my little finger in his mouth, as I had seen women do to quiet their babies, and his suck was eager.

"He's hungry," I said urgently, "wake up and feed him."

But Adelaide rolled over and turned her face to the wall.

MILK CAME FLOODING into Adelaide's breasts, more than the baby could drink at first. She had to feed him. Milk leaked out in dark patches on her pale-blue shirtwaists. She moved heavily, burdened by the ache. She did not completely ignore the baby. She cut her skirts up for diapers, sewed a layette from her nightgown, but at the same time she only grudgingly cared for his basic needs, and often left him to howl. Sometimes he cried such a long time that the landlady came puffing upstairs to see what was wrong. I think she was troubled to see us in such desperation, because she silently brought up food left by the boarders who paid for meals. Nevertheless, she did not change her decision. When the two weeks were up, we still had to move.

Spring was faintly in the air the day we went out looking for a new place. The clouds were high and warm. All of the everyday clothes Adelaide owned had been cut up for the baby, so she had nothing but her fine things, lace and silk, good cashmere. She wore a black coat, a pale green dress trimmed in cream lace, and delicate string gloves. Her beautiful hair was pinned back in a strict knot. We walked down the brick sidewalks looking for signs in windows, for rooming houses of the cheapest kind, barracks, or hotels. We found nothing, and finally sat down to rest on a bench bolted to the side of a store. In those times, the streets of towns were much kindlier. No one minded the destitute gathering strength, taking a load off, discussing their downfall in the world.

"We can't go back to Fritzie," Adelaide said, "I couldn't bear to live with Pete."

"We have nowhere else," I sensibly told her, "unless you sell your heirlooms."

Adelaide gave me a warning look and put her hand to the brooch at her throat. I stopped. She was attached to the few precious treasures she often showed us – the complicated garnet necklace, the onyx mourning brooch, the ring with the good yellow diamond. I supposed that she wouldn't sell them even to save us. Our hardship had beaten her and she was weak, but in her weakness she was also stubborn. We sat on the store's bench for perhaps half an hour, then Karl noticed something like music in the air.

"Mama," he begged, "Mama, can we go? It's a fair!"

As always with Karl, she began by saying no, but that was just a formality and both of them knew it. In no time, he had wheedled and charmed her into going.

The Orphan's Picnic, a fair held to benefit the orphans of Saint Jerome's after the long winter, was taking place just a few streets over at the city fairground. We saw the banner blazing cheerful red, stretched across the entrance, bearing the seal of the patron saint of loneliness. Plank booths were set up in the long, brown winter grass. Cowled nuns switched busily between the scapular and holy medal counters, or stood poised behind racks of rosaries, shoeboxes full of holy cards, tiny carved statuettes of saints, and common toys. We swept into the excitement, looked over the grab bags, games of chance, displays of candy and religious wares. Adelaide stopped at a secular booth that sold jingling hardware, and pulled a whole dollar from her purse.

"I'll take that," she said to the vendor, pointing. He lifted a pearl-handled jackknife from his case and Mama gave it to Karl. Then she pointed at a bead necklace, silver and gold.

"I don't want it," I said to Adelaide.

Her face reddened, but after a slight hesitation she bought the necklace anyway. Then she had Karl fasten it around her throat. She put the baby in my arms.

"Here, Miss Damp Blanket," she said.

Karl laughed and took her hand. Meandering from booth to booth, we finally came to the grandstand, and at once Karl began to pull her toward the seats, drawn by the excitement. I had to stumble along behind them. Bills littered the ground. Posters were pasted up the sides of trees and the splintery walls. Adelaide picked up one of the smaller papers.

THE GREAT OMAR, it said, AERONAUT EXTRAORDINAIRE.

APPEARING HERE AT NOON. Below the words there was a picture of a man – sleek, mustachioed, yellow scarf whipping in a breeze.

"Please," Karl said, "please!"

And so we joined the gaping crowd.

The plane dipped, rolled, buzzed, glided above us and I was no more impressed than if it had been some sort of insect. I did not crane my neck or gasp, thrilled, like the rest of them. I looked down at the baby and watched his face. He was just emerging from the newborn's endless sleep and from time to time now he stared fathomlessly into my eyes. I stared back. Looking into his face that day, I found a different arrangement of myself – bolder, quick as light, ill-tempered. He frowned at me, unafraid, unaware that he was helpless, only troubled at the loud drone of the biplane as it landed and taxied toward us on the field.

Thinking back now, I can't believe that I had no premonition of what power The Great Omar had over us. I hardly glanced when he jumped from the plane and I did not applaud his sweeping bows and pronouncements. I hardly knew when he offered rides to those who dared. I believe he charged a dollar or two for the privilege. I did not notice. I was hardly prepared for what came next.

"Here!" my mother called, holding her purse up in the sun.

Then without a backwards look, without a word, with no warning and no hesitation, she elbowed through the crowd collected at the base of the grandstand and stepped into the cleared space around the pilot. That was when I looked at The Great Omar for the first time, but, as I was so astonished at my mother, I can hardly recall any detail of his appearance. The general impression he gave was dashing, like his posters. The yellow scarf whipped out and certainly he had some sort of moustache. I believe he wore a grease-stained white sweater, perhaps a loose coverall. He was slender and dark, much smaller in relation to his plane than the poster showed, and older. After he helped my mother into the passenger's cockpit and jumped in behind the controls, he pulled a pair of green goggles down over his face. And then there was a startling, endless moment, as they prepared for the takeoff.

"Clear prop!"

The propeller made a wind. The plane lurched forward, lifted over the low trees, gained height. The Great Omar circled the field in a low swoop and I saw my mother's long red crinkly hair spring from its tight knot and float free in an arc that seemed to reach out and tangle around his shoulders.

Karl stared in stricken fascination at the sky, and said nothing as The Great Omar began his stunts and droning passes. I did not watch. Again, I fixed my gaze on the face of my little brother and concentrated on his features, blind to the possibilities of Adelaide's sudden liftoff. I only wanted her to come back down before the plane smashed.

The crowd thinned. People drifted away, but I did not notice. By the time I looked into the sky, The Great Omar was flying steadily away from the fairgrounds with my mother. Soon the plane was only a white dot, then it blended into the pale blue sky and vanished.

I shook Karl's arm but he pulled away from me and vaulted to the edge of the grandstand. "Take me!" he screamed, leaning over the rail. He stared at the sky, poised as if he'd throw himself into it.

Satisfaction. That was the first thing I felt after Adelaide flew off. For once she had played no favorites between Karl and me, but left us both. So there was some compensation in what she did. Karl threw his head in his hands and began to sob into his heavy wool sleeves. Only then did I feel frightened.

Below the grandstand, the crowd moved in patternless waves. Over us the clouds spread into a thin sheet that covered the sky like muslin. We watched the dusk collect in the corners of the field. Nuns began to pack away their rosaries and prayer books. Colored lights went on in the little nonreligious booths. Karl slapped his arms, stamped his feet, blew on his fingers. He was more sensitive to cold than I. Huddling around the baby kept me warm.

The baby woke, very hungry, and I was helpless to comfort him. He sucked so hard that my finger was white and puckered, and then he screamed. People gathered around us there. Women held out their arms, but I did not give the baby to any of them. I did not trust them. I did not trust the man who sat down beside me, either, and spoke softly. He was a young man with a hard-boned, sad, unshaven face. What I remember most about him was the sadness. He wanted to take the baby back to his wife so she could feed him. She had a new baby of her own, he said, and enough milk for two.

"I am waiting," I said, "for our own mother."

"When is she coming back?" asked the young man.

I could not answer. The sad man waited with open arms. Karl sat mute on one side of me, gazing into the dark sky. Behind and before, large interfering ladies counseled and conferred.

"Give him the baby, dear."

"Don't be stubborn."

"Let him take the baby home."

"No," I said to every order and suggestion. I even kicked hard when one woman tried to take my brother from my arms. They grew discouraged, or simply indifferent after a time, and went off. It was not the ladies who convinced me, finally, but the baby himself. He did not let up screaming. The longer he cried, the longer the sad man sat beside me, the weaker my resistance was, until finally I could barely hold my own tears back.

"I'm coming with you then," I told the young man. "I'll bring the baby back here when he's fed."

"No," cried Karl, coming out of his stupor suddenly, "you can't leave me alone!"

He grabbed my arm so fervently that the baby slipped, and then the young man caught me, as if to help, but instead he scooped the baby to himself.

"I'll take care of him," he said, and turned away.

I tried to wrench from Karl's grip, but like my mother he was strongest when he was weak, and I could not break free. I saw the man walk into the shadows. I heard the baby's wail fade. I finally sat down beside Karl and let the cold sink into me.

One hour passed. Another hour. When the colored lights went out and the moon came up, diffused behind the sheets of clouds, I knew the young man wasn't coming back. And yet, because he looked too sad to do any harm to anyone, I was more afraid for Karl and myself. We were the ones who were thoroughly lost. I stood up. Karl stood with me. Without a word we walked down the empty streets to our old rooming house. We had no key but Karl displayed one unexpected talent. He took the thin-bladed knife that Adelaide had given him, and picked the lock.

Once we stood in the cold room, the sudden presence of our mother's clothing dismayed us. The room was filled with the faint perfume of the dried flowers that she scattered in her trunk, the rich scent of the clove-studded orange she hung in the closet and the lavender oil she rubbed into her skin at night. The sweetness of her breath seemed to linger, the rustle of her silk underskirt, the quick sound of her heels. Our longing buried us. We sank down on her bed and cried, wrapped in her quilt, clutching each other. When that was done, however, I acquired a brain of ice.

I washed my face in the basin, then I roused Karl and told him we were going to Aunt Fritzie's. He acquiesced, suffering again in a dumb lethargy. We ate all there was to eat in the room, two cold pancakes, and packed what we owned in a small cardboard suitcase. Karl carried that. I carried the quilt. The last thing I did was reach far back in my mother's drawer and pull out her small round keepsake box. It was covered in blue velvet and tightly locked.

"We might need to sell these things," I told Karl. He hesitated but then, with a hard look, he took the box.

We slipped out before sunrise and walked to the train station. In the weedy yards there were men who knew each boxcar's destination. We found the car we wanted and climbed in. There was hay in one corner. We spread the quilt over it and rolled up together, curled tight, with our heads on the suitcase and Adelaide's blue velvet box between us in Karl's breast pocket. We clung to the thought of the treasures inside of it.

We spent a day and a night on that train while it switched and braked and rumbled on an agonizingly complex route to Argus. We did not dare jump off for a drink of water or to scavenge food. The one time we did try this the train started up so quickly that we were hardly able to catch the side rungs again. We lost our suitcase and the quilt because we took the wrong car, farther back, and that night we did not sleep at all for the cold. Karl was too miserable even to argue with me when I told him it was my turn to hold Adelaide's box. I put it in the bodice of my jumper. It did not keep me warm, but even so, the sparkle of the diamond when I shut my eyes, the patterns of garnets that whirled in the dark air, gave me something. My mind hardened, faceted and gleaming like a magic stone, and I saw my mother clearly.

She was still in the plane, flying close to the pulsing stars, when suddenly Omar noticed that the fuel was getting low. He did not love Adelaide at first sight, or even care what happened to her. He had to save himself. Somehow he had to lighten his load. So he set his controls. He stood up in his cockpit. Then in one sud- den motion he plucked my mother out of her seat like a doll and dropped her overboard.

All night she fell through the awful cold. Her coat flapped open and her pale green dress wrapped tightly around her legs. Her red hair flowed straight upward like a flame. She was a candle that gave no warmth. My heart froze. I had no love for her. That is why, by morning, I allowed her to hit the earth.

By the time we saw the sign on the brick station, I was dull again, a block of sullen cold. Still, it hurt when I jumped, scraping my cold knees and the heels of my hands. The pain sharpened me enough to read signs in windows and rack my mind for just where Aunt Fritzie's shop was. It had been years since we visited.

Karl was older, and I probably should not hold myself accountable for losing him too. But I didn't call him. I didn't run after him. I couldn't stand how his face glowed in the blossoms' reflected light, pink and radiant, so like the way he sat beneath our mother's stroking hand.

When I stopped running, I realized I was alone and now more truly lost than any of my family, since all I had done from the first was to try and hold them close while death, panic, chance, and ardor each took them their separate ways.

Hot tears came up suddenly behind my eyes and my ears burned. I ached to cry, hard, but I knew that was useless and so I walked. I walked carefully, looking at everything around me, and it was lucky I did this because I'd run past the butcher shop and, suddenly, there it was, set back from the road down a short dirt drive. A white pig was painted on the side, and inside the pig, the lettering "Kozka's Meats." I walked toward it between rows of tiny fir trees. The place looked both shabby and prosperous, as though Fritzie and Pete were too busy with customers to care for outward appearances. I stood on the broad front stoop and noticed everything I could, the way a beggar does. A rack of elk horns was nailed overhead. I walked beneath them.

The entryway was dark, my heart was in my throat. And then, what I saw was quite natural, understandable, although it was not real.

Again, the dog leapt toward Karl and blossoms from his stick fell. Except that they fell around me in the entrance to the store. I smelled the petals melting on my coat, tasted their thin sweetness in my mouth. I had no time to wonder how this could be happening because they disappeared as suddenly as they'd come when I told my name to the man behind the glass counter.

This man, tall and fat with a pale brown moustache and an old blue denim cap on his head, was Uncle Pete. His eyes were round, mild, exactly the same light brown as his hair. His smile was slow, sweet for a butcher, and always hopeful. He did not recognize me even after I told him who I was. Finally his eyes widened and he called out for Fritzie.

"Your sister's girl! She's here!" he shouted down the hall.

I told him I was alone, that I had come in on the boxcar, and he lifted me up in his arms. He carried me back to the kitchen where Aunt Fritzie was frying a sausage for my cousin, the beautiful Sita, who sat at the table and stared at me with narrowed eyes while I tried to tell Fritzie and Pete just how I'd come to walk into their front door out of nowhere.

They stared at me with friendly suspicion, thinking that I'd run away. But when I told them about The Great Omar, and how Adelaide held up her purse, and how Omar helped her into the plane, their faces turned grim.

"Sita, go polish the glass out front," said Aunt Fritzie. Sita slid unwillingly out of her chair. "Now," Fritzie said. Uncle Pete sat down heavily. The ends of his moustache went into his mouth, he pressed his thumbs together under his chin, and turned to me. "Go on, tell the rest," he said, and so I told all of the rest, and when I had finished I saw that I had also drunk a glass of milk and eaten a sausage. By then I could hardly sit upright. Uncle Pete took me in his strong arms and I remember sagging against him, then nothing. I slept that day and all night and did not wake until the next morning. Sleep robbed me as profoundly as being awake had, for when I finally woke I had no memory of where I was and how I'd got there. I lay still for what seemed like a long while, trying to place the objects in the room.

This was the room where I would sleep for the rest of my childhood, or what passed for childhood anyway, since after that train journey I was not a child. It was a pleasant room, and before me it belonged entirely to cousin Sita. The paneling was warm-stained pine. Most of the space was taken up by a tall oak dresser with fancy curlicues and many drawers. A small sheet of polished tin hung on the door and served as a mirror. Through that door, as I was trying to understand my surroundings, walked Sita herself, tall and perfect with a blond braid that reached to her waist.

"So you're finally awake." She sat down on the edge of my trundle bed and folded her arms over her small new breasts. She was a year older than me. Since I'd seen her last, she had grown suddenly, like Karl, but her growth had not thinned her into an awkward bony creature. She was now a slim female of utter grace.

I realized I was staring too long at her, and then the whole series of events came flooding back and I turned away. Sita grinned. She looked down at me, her strong white teeth shining, and she stroked the blond braid that hung down over one shoulder.

"Where's Auntie Adelaide?" she asked.

I did not answer.

"Where's Auntie Adelaide?" she asked, again. "How come you came here? Where'd she go? Where's Karl?"

"I don't know."

I suppose I thought the misery of my answer would quiet Sita but that was before I knew her. It only fueled more questions.

"How come Auntie left you alone? Where's Karl? What's this?"

She took the blue velvet box from my pile of clothes and shook it casually next to her ear.

"What's in it?"

For the moment at least, I bested her by snatching the box with an angry swiftness she did not expect. I rolled from the bed, bundled my clothes into my arms, and walked out of the room. The one door open in the hallway was the bathroom, a large smoky room of many uses that soon became my haven since it was the only door I could bolt against my cousin.

EVERY DAY for weeks after I arrived in Argus, I woke up thinking I was back on the farm with my mother and father and that none of this had happened. I always managed to believe this until I opened my eyes. Then I saw the dark swirls in the pine and Sita's arm hanging off the bed above me. I smelled the air, peppery and warm from the sausage makers. I heard the rhythmical whine of meat saws, slicers, the rippling beat of fans. Aunt Fritzie was smoking her sharp Viceroys in the bathroom. Uncle

Pete was outside feeding the big white German shepherd that was kept in the shop at night to guard the canvas bags of money.

Every morning I got up, put on one of Sita's hand-me-down pink dresses, and went out to the kitchen to wait for Uncle Pete. I cooked breakfast. That I made fried eggs and a good cup of coffee at age eleven was a source of wonder to my aunt and uncle, and an outrage to Sita. That's why I did it every morning, with a finesse that got more casual until it became a habit to have me there.

From the first I made myself essential. I did this because I had to, because I had nothing else to offer. The day after I arrived in Argus and woke up to Sita's calculating smile I also tried to offer what I thought was treasure, the blue velvet box that held Adelaide's heirlooms.

I did it in as grand a manner as I could, with Sita for a witness and with Pete and Fritzie sitting at the kitchen table. That morning, I walked in with my hair combed wet and laid the box between the two of them. I looked at Sita as I spoke.

"This should pay my way."

Fritzie looked at me. She had my mother's features sharpened one notch past beauty. Her skin was rough and her short curled hair was yellow, bleached pale, not golden. Fritzie's eyes were a swimming, crazy shade of blue that startled customers. She ate heartily, but her constant smoking kept her string-bean thin and sallow.

"You don't have to pay us," said Fritzie, "Pete, tell her. She doesn't have to pay us. Sit down, shut up, and eat."

Fritzie spoke like that, joking and blunt. Pete was slower. "Come. Sit down and forget about the money," he said. "You never know about your mother..." he added in an earnest voice that trailed away when he looked at Aunt Fritzie. Things had a way of evaporating under her eyes, vanishing, getting sucked up into the blue heat of her stare. Even Sita had nothing to say.

"I want to give you this," I said. "I insist."

"She insists," exclaimed Aunt Fritzie. Her smile had a rakish flourish because one tooth was chipped in front. "Don't insist," she said. "Eat."

But I would not sit down. I took a knife from the butter plate and started to pry the lock up.

"Here now," said Fritzie. "Pete, help her."

So Pete got up slowly and fetched a screwdriver from the top of the icebox and sat down and jammed the end underneath the lock.

"Let her open it," said Fritzie, when the lock popped up. So Pete pushed the little round box across the table.

"I bet it's empty," Sita said. She took a big chance saying that, but it paid off in spades and aces between us growing up, because I lifted the lid a moment later and what she said was true. There was nothing of value in the box.

Stick pins. A few thick metal buttons off a coat. And a ticket describing the necklace of tiny garnets, pawned for practically nothing in Minneapolis.

There was silence. Even Fritzie was at a loss. Sita nearly buzzed off her chair in triumph but held her tongue, that is until later, when she would crow. Pete put his hand on his head in deep vexation. I stood quietly, stunned.

What is dark is light and bad news brings slow gain, I told myself. I could see a pattern to all of what happened, a pattern that suggested completion in years to come. The baby was lifted up while my mother was dashed to earth. Karl rode west and I ran east. It is opposites that finally meet.

ALICE MUNRO

Walker Brothers Cowboy

AFTER SUPPER my father says, "Want to go down and see if the Lake's still there?" We leave my mother sewing under the dining room light, making clothes for me against the opening of school. She has ripped up for this purpose an old suit and an old plaid wool dress of hers, and she has to cut and match very cleverly and also make me stand and turn for endless fittings, sweaty, itching from the hot wool, ungrateful. We leave my brother in bed in the little screened porch at the end of the front verandah, and sometimes he kneels on his bed and presses his face against the screen and calls mournfully, "Bring me an ice cream cone!" but I call back, "You will be asleep," and do not even turn my head.

Then my father and I walk gradually down a long, shabby sort of street, with Silverwoods Ice Cream signs standing on the sidewalk, outside tiny, lighted stores. This is in Tuppertown, an old town on Lake Huron, an old grain port. The street is shaded, in some places, by maple trees whose roots have cracked and heaved the sidewalk and spread out like crocodiles into the bare yards. People are sitting out, men in shirt-sleeves and undershirts and women in aprons – not people we know but if anybody looks ready to nod and say, "Warm night," my father will nod too and say something the same. Children are still playing. I don't know them either because my mother keeps my brother and me in our own yard, saying he is too young to leave it and I have to mind him. I am not so sad to watch their evening games because the games themselves are ragged, dissolving. Children, of their own will, draw apart, separate into islands of two or one under the heavy trees, occupying themselves in such solitary ways as I do all day, planting pebbles in the dirt or writing in it with a stick.

Presently we leave these yards and houses behind, we pass a factory with boarded-up windows, a lumberyard whose high wooden gates are locked for the night. Then the town falls away in a defeated jumble of sheds and small junkyards, the sidewalk gives up and we are walking on a sandy path with burdocks, plantains, humble nameless weeds all around. We enter a vacant lot, a kind of park really, for it is kept clear of junk and there is one bench with a slat missing on the back, a place to sit and look at the water. Which is generally grey in the evening, under a lightly overcast sky, no sunsets, the horizon dim. A very quiet, washing noise on the stones of the beach. Farther along, towards the main part of town, there is a stretch of sand, a water slide, floats bobbing around the safe swimming area, a life guard's rickety throne. Also a long dark green building, like a roofed verandah, called the Pavilion, full of farmers and their wives, in stiff good clothes, on Sundays. That is the part of the town we used to know when we lived at Dungannon and came here three or four times a summer, to the Lake. That, and the docks where we would go and look at the grain boats, ancient, rusty, wallowing, making us wonder how they got past the breakwater let alone to Fort William.

Tramps hang around the docks and occasionally on these evenings wander up the dwindling beach and climb the shifting, precarious path boys have made, hanging onto dry bushes, and say something to my father which, being frightened of tramps, I am too alarmed to catch. My father says he is a bit hard up himself. "I'll roll you a cigarette if it's any use to you," he says, and he shakes tobacco out carefully on one of the thin butterfly papers, flicks it with his tongue, seals it and hands it to the tramp who takes it and walks away. My father also rolls and lights and smokes one cigarette of his own.

He tells me how the Great Lakes came to be. All where Lake Huron is now, he says, used to be flat land, a wide flat plain. Then came the ice, creeping down from the north, pushing deep into the low places. Like *that* – and he shows me his hand with his spread fingers pressing the rock-hard ground where we are sitting. His fingers make hardly any impression at all and he says, "Well, the old ice cap had a lot more power behind it than this hand has." And then the ice went back, shrank back towards the North Pole where it came from, and left its fingers of ice in the deep places it had gouged, and ice turned to lakes and there they were today. They were *new*, as time went. I try to see that plain before me, dinosaurs walking on it, but I am not able even to imagine the shore of the Lake when the Indians were there, before Tuppertown. The tiny share we have of time appalls me, though my father seems to regard it with tranquillity. Even my father, who sometimes seems to me to have been at home in the world as long as it has lasted, has really lived on this earth only a little longer than I have, in terms of all the time there has been to live in. He has not known a time, any more than I, when automobiles and electric lights did not at least exist. He was not alive when this century started. I will be barely alive – old, old – when it ends. I do not like to think of it. I wish the Lake to be always just a lake, with the safe-swimming floats marking it, and the breakwater and the lights of Tuppertown.

My father has a job, selling for Walker Brothers. This is a firm that sells almost entirely in the country, the back country. Sunshine, Boylesbridge, Turnaround – that is all his territory. Not Dungannon where we used to live, Dungannon is too near town and my mother is grateful for that. He sells cough medicine, iron tonic, corn plasters, laxatives, pills for female disorders, mouth wash, shampoo, liniment, salves, lemon and orange and raspberry concentrate for making refreshing drinks, vanilla, food colouring, black and green tea, ginger, cloves and other spices, rat poison. He has a song about it, with these two lines:

And have all liniments and oils,
For everything from corns to boils...

Not a very funny song, in my mother's opinion. A pedlar's song, and that is what he is, a pedlar knocking at backwoods kitchens. Up until last winter we had our own business, a fox farm. My father raised silver foxes and sold their pelts to the people who make them into capes and coats and muffs. Prices fell, my father hung on hoping they would get better next year, and they fell again, and he hung on one more year and one more and finally it was not possible to hang on any more, we owed everything to the feed company. I have heard my mother explain this, several times, to Mrs. Oliphant who is the only neighbour she talks to. (Mrs. Oliphant also has come down in the world, being a schoolteacher who married the janitor.) We poured all we had into it, my mother says, and we came out with nothing. Many people could say the same thing, these days, but my mother has no time for the national calamity, only ours. Fate has flung us onto a street of poor people (it does not matter that we were poor before, that was a different sort of poverty), and the only way to take this, as she sees it, is with dignity, with bitterness, with no reconciliation. No bathroom with a claw-footed tub and a flush toilet is going to comfort her, nor water on tap and sidewalks past the house and milk in bottles, not even the two movie theatres and the Venus Restaurant and Woolworths so marvellous it has live birds singing in its fan-cooled corners and fish as tiny as fingernails, as bright as moons, swimming in its green tanks. My mother does not care.

In the afternoons she often walks to Simon's Grocery and takes me with her to help carry things. She wears a good dress, navy blue with little flowers, sheer, worn over a navy-blue slip. Also a summer hat of white straw, pushed down on the side of the head, and white shoes I have just whitened on a newspaper on the back steps. I have my hair freshly done in long damp curls which the dry air will fortunately soon loosen, a stiff large hair-ribbon on top of my head. This is entirely different from going out after supper with my father. We have not walked past two houses before I feel we have become objects of universal ridicule. Even the dirty words chalked on the sidewalks are laughing at us. My mother does not seem to notice. She walks serenely like a lady shopping, like a *lady* shopping, past the housewives in loose beltless dresses torn under the arms. With me her creation, wretched curls and flaunting hair bow, scrubbed knees and white socks – all I do not want to be. I loathe even my name when she says it in public, in a voice so high, proud and ringing, deliberately different from the voice of any other mother on the street.

My mother will sometimes carry home, for a treat, a brick of ice cream – pale Neapolitan; and because we have no refrigerator in our house we wake my brother and eat it at once in the dining room, always darkened by the wall of the house next door. I spoon it up tenderly, leaving the chocolate till last, hoping to have some still to eat when my brother's dish is empty. My mother tries then to imitate the conversations we used to have at Dungannon, going back to our earliest, most leisurely days before my brother was born, when she would give me a little tea and a lot of milk in a cup like hers and we would sit out on the step facing the pump, the lilac tree, the fox pens beyond. She is not able to keep from mentioning those days. "Do you remember when we put you in your sled and Major pulled you?" (Major, our dog, that we had to leave with neighbours when we moved.) "Do you remember your sandbox outside the kitchen window?" I pretend to remember far less than I do, wary of being trapped into sympathy or any unwanted emotion.

My mother has headaches. She often has to lie down. She lies on my brother's narrow bed in the little screened porch, shaded by heavy branches. "I look up at that tree and I think I am at home," she says.

"What you need," my father tells her, "is some fresh air and a drive in the country." He means for her to go with him, on his Walker Brothers route.

That is not my mother's idea of a drive in the country.

"Can I come?"

"Your mother might want you for trying on clothes."

"I'm beyond sewing this afternoon," my mother says.

"I'll take her then. Take both of them, give you a rest."

What is there about us that people need to be given a rest from? Never mind. I am glad enough to find my brother and make him go to the toilet and get us both into the car, our knees unscrubbed, my hair unringleted. My father brings from the house his two heavy brown suitcases, full of bottles, and sets them on the back seat. He wears a white shirt, brilliant in the sunlight, a tie, light trousers belonging to his summer suit (his other suit is black, for funerals, and belonged to my uncle before he died) and a creamy straw hat. His salesman's outfit, with pencils clipped in the shirt pocket. He goes back once again, probably to say good-bye to my mother, to ask her if she is sure she doesn't want to come, and hear her say, "No. No thanks, I'm better just to lie here with my eyes closed." Then we are backing out of the driveway with the rising hope of adventure, just the little hope that takes you over the bump into the street, the hot air starting to move, turning into a breeze, the houses growing less and less familiar as we follow the short cut my father knows, the quick way out of town. Yet what is there waiting for us all afternoon but hot hours in stricken farmyards, perhaps a stop at a country store and three ice cream cones or bottles of pop, and my father singing? The one he made up about himself has a title – "The Walker Brothers Cowboy" – and it starts out like this:

Old Ned Fields, he now is dead,
So I am ridin' the route instead…

Who is Ned Fields? The man he has replaced, surely, and if so he really is dead; yet my father's voice is mournful-jolly, making his death some kind of nonsense, a comic calamity. "Wisht I was back on the Rio Grande, plungin' through the dusky sand." My father sings most of the time while driving the car. Even now, heading out of town, crossing the bridge and taking the sharp turn onto the highway, he is humming something, mumbling a bit of a song to himself, just tuning up, really, getting ready to improvise, for out along the highway we pass the Baptist Camp, the Vacation Bible Camp, and he lets loose:

Where are the Baptists, where are the Baptists,
where are all the Baptists today?
They're down in the water, in Lake Huron water,
with their sins all a-gittin' washed away.

My brother takes this for straight truth and gets up on his knees trying to see down to the Lake. "I don't see any Baptists," he says accusingly. "Neither do I, son," says my father. "I told you, they're down in the Lake."

No roads paved when we left the highway. We have to roll up the windows because of dust. The land is flat, scorched, empty. Bush lots at the back of the farms hold shade, black pine-shade like pools nobody can ever get to. We bump up a long lane and at the end of it what could look more unwelcoming, more deserted than the tall unpainted farmhouse with grass growing uncut right up to the front door, green blinds down and a door upstairs opening on nothing but air? Many houses have this door, and I have never yet been able to find out why. I ask my father and he says they are for walking in your sleep. *What?* Well if you happen to be walking in your sleep and you want to step outside. I am offended, seeing too late that he is joking, as usual, but my brother says sturdily, "If they did that they would break their necks."

The nineteen-thirties. How much this kind of farmhouse, this kind of afternoon, seem to me to belong to that one decade in time, just as my father's hat does, his bright flared tie, our car with its wide running board (an Essex, and long past its prime). Cars somewhat like it, many older, none dustier, sit in the farmyards. Some are past running and have their doors pulled off, their seats removed for use on porches. No living things to be seen, chickens or cattle. Except dogs. There are dogs, lying in any kind of shade they can find, dreaming, their lean sides rising and sinking rapidly. They get up when my father opens the car door, he has to speak to them. "Nice boy, there's a boy, nice old boy." They quiet down, go back to their shade. He should know how to quiet animals, he has held desperate foxes with tongs around their necks. One gentling voice for the dogs and another, rousing, cheerful, for calling at doors. "Hello there, Missus, it's the Walker Brothers man and what are you out of today?" A door opens, he disappears. Forbidden to follow, forbidden even to leave the car, we can just wait and wonder what he says. Sometimes trying to make my mother laugh he pretends to be himself in a farm kitchen, spreading out his sample case. "Now then, Missus, are you troubled with parasitic life? Your children's scalps, I mean. All those crawly little things we're too polite to mention that show up on the heads of the best of families? Soap alone is useless, kerosene is not too nice a perfume, but I have here – " Or else, "Believe me, sitting and driving all day the way I do I *know* the value of these fine pills. Natural relief. A problem common to old folks, too, once their days of activity are over – How about you, Grandma?" He would wave the imaginary box of pills under my mother's nose and she would laugh finally, unwillingly. "He doesn't say that really, does he?" I said, and she said no of course not, he was too much of a gentleman.

One yard after another, then, the old cars, the pumps, dogs, views of grey barns and falling-down sheds and unturning windmills. The men, if they are working in the fields, are not in any fields that we can see. The children are far away, following dry creek beds or looking for blackberries, or else they are hidden in the house, spying at us through cracks in the blinds. The car seat has grown slick with our sweat. I dare my brother to sound the horn, wanting to do it myself but not wanting to get the blame. He knows better. We play *I Spy*, but it is hard to find many colours. Grey for the barns and sheds and toilets and houses, brown for the yard and fields, black or brown for the dogs. The rusting cars show rainbow patches, in which I strain to pick out purple or green; likewise I peer at doors for shreds of old peeling paint, maroon or yellow. We can't play with letters, which would be better, because my brother is too young to spell. The game disintegrates anyway. He claims my colours are not fair, and wants extra turns.

In one house no door opens, though the car is in the yard. My father knocks and whistles, calls, "Hullo there! Walker Brothers man!" but there is not a stir of reply anywhere. This house has no porch, just a bare, slanting slab of cement on which my father stands. He turns around, searching the barnyard, the barn whose mow must be empty because you can see the sky through it, and finally he bends to pick up his suitcases. Just then a window is opened upstairs, a white pot appears on the sill, is tilted over and its contents splash down the outside wall. The window is not directly above my father's head, so only a stray splash would catch him. He picks up his suitcases with no particular hurry and walks, no longer whistling, to the car. "Do you know what that was?" I say to my brother. "*Pee.*" He laughs and laughs.

My father rolls and lights a cigarette before he starts the car. The window has been slammed down, the blind drawn, we never did see a hand or face. "Pee, pee," sings my brother ecstatically. "Somebody dumped down pee!" "Just don't tell your mother that," my father says. "She isn't liable to see the joke." "Is it in your song?" my brother wants to know. My father says no but he will see what he can do to work it in.

I notice in a little while that we are not turning in any more lanes, though it does not seem to me that we are headed home.

"Is this the way to Sunshine?" I ask my father, and he answers, "No ma'am it's not."

"Are we still in your territory?" He shakes his head. "We're going *fast*," my brother says approvingly, and in fact we are bouncing along through dry puddleholes so that all the bottles in the suitcases clink together and gurgle promisingly.

Another lane, a house, also unpainted, dried to silver in the sun.

"I thought we were out of your territory."

"We are."

"Then what are we going in here for?"

"You'll see."

In front of the house a short, sturdy woman is picking up washing, which had been spread on the grass to bleach and dry. When the car stops she stares at it hard for a moment, bends to pick up a couple more towels to add to the bundle under her arm, comes across to us and says in a flat voice, neither welcoming nor unfriendly, "Have you lost your way?"

My father takes his time getting out of the car. "I don't think so," he says. "I'm the Walker Brothers man."

"George Golley is our Walker Brothers man," the woman says, "and he was out here no more than a week ago. Oh, my Lord God," she says harshly, "it's you."

"It was, the last time I looked in the mirror," my father says. The woman gathers all the towels in front of her and holds on to them tightly, pushing them against her stomach as if it hurt.

"Of all the people I never thought to see. And telling me you were the Walker Brothers man."

"I'm sorry if you were looking forward to George Golley," my father says humbly.

"And look at me, I was prepared to clean the hen-house. You'll think that's just an excuse but it's true. I don't go round looking like this every day." She is wearing a farmer's straw hat, through which pricks of sunlight penetrate and float on her face, a loose, dirty print smock and running shoes. "Who are those in the car, Ben? They're not yours?"

"Well I hope and believe they are," my father says, and tells our names and ages. "Come on, you can get out. This is Nora, Miss Cronin. Nora, you better tell me, is it still Miss, or have you got a husband hiding in the woodshed?"

"If I had a husband that's not where I'd keep him, Ben," she says, and they both laugh, her laugh abrupt and somewhat angry. "You'll think I got no manners, as well as being dressed like a tramp," she says. "Come on in out of the sun. It's cool in the house."

We go across the yard ("Excuse me taking you in this way but I don't think the front door has been opened since Papa's funeral, I'm afraid the hinges might drop off"), up the porch steps, into the kitchen, which really is cool, high-ceilinged, the blinds of course down, a simple, clean, threadbare room with waxed worn linoleum, potted geraniums, drinking-pail and dipper, a round table with scrubbed oilcloth. In spite of the cleanness, the wiped and swept surfaces, there is a faint sour smell – maybe of the dishrag or the tin dipper or the oilcloth, or the old lady, because there is one, sitting in an easy chair under the clock shelf. She turns her head slightly in our direction and says, "Nora? Is that company?"

"Blind," says Nora in a quick explaining voice to my father. Then, "You won't guess who it is, Momma. Hear his voice."

My father goes to the front of her chair and bends and says hopefully, "Afternoon, Mrs. Cronin."

"Ben Jordan," says the old lady with no surprise. "You haven't been to see us in the longest time. Have you been out of the country?"

My father and Nora look at each other.

"He's married, Momma," says Nora cheerfully and aggressively. "Married and got two children and here they are." She pulls us forward, makes each of us touch the old lady's dry, cool hand while she says our names in turn. Blind! This is the first blind person I have ever seen close up. Her eyes are closed, the eyelids sunk away down, showing no shape of the eyeball, just hollows. From one hollow comes a drop of silver liquid, a medicine, or a miraculous tear.

"Let me get into a decent dress," Nora says. "Talk to Momma. It's a treat for her. We hardly ever see company, do we Momma?"

"Not many makes it out this road," says the old lady placidly. "And the ones that used to be around here, our old neighbours, some of them have pulled out."

"True everywhere," my father says.

"Where's your wife then?"

"Home. She's not too fond of the hot weather, makes her feel poorly."

"Well." This is a habit of country people, old people, to say "well," meaning, "is that so?" with a little extra politeness and concern.

Nora's dress, when she appears again – stepping heavily on Cuban heels down the stairs in the hall – is flowered more lavishly than anything my mother owns, green and yellow on brown, some sort of floating sheer crepe, leaving her arms bare. Her arms are heavy, and every bit of her skin you can see is covered with little dark freckles like measles. Her hair is short, black, coarse and curly, her teeth very white and strong. "It's the first time I knew there was such a thing as green poppies," my father says, looking at her dress.

"You would be surprised all the things you never knew," says Nora, sending a smell of cologne far and wide when she moves and displaying a change of voice to go with the dress, something more sociable and youthful. "They're not poppies anyway, they're just flowers. You go and pump me some good cold water and I'll make these children a drink." She gets down from the cupboard a bottle of Walker Brothers orange syrup.

"You telling me you were the Walker Brothers man!"

"It's the truth, Nora. You go and look at my sample cases in the car if you don't believe me. I got the territory directly south of here."

"Walker Brothers? Is that a fact? You selling for Walker Brothers?"

"Yes ma'am."

"We always heard you were raising foxes over Dungannon way."

"That's what I was doing, but I kind of run out of luck in that business."

"So where're you living? How long've you been out selling?"

"We moved into Tuppertown. I been at it, oh, two, three months. It keeps the wolf man from the door. Keeps him as far away as the back fence."

Nora laughs. "Well I guess you count yourself lucky to have the work. Isabel's husband in Brantford, he was out of work the longest time. I thought if he didn't find something soon I was going to have them all land in here to feed, and I tell you I was hardly looking forward to it. It's all I can manage with me and Momma."

"Isabel married," my father says. "Muriel married too?"

"No, she's teaching school out west. She hasn't been home for five years. I guess she finds something better to do with her holidays. I would if I was her." She gets some snapshots out of the table drawer and starts showing him. "That's Isabel's oldest boy, starting school. That's the baby sitting in her carriage. Isabel and her husband. Muriel. That's her roommate with her. That's a fellow she used to go around with, and his car. He was working in a bank out there. That's her school, it has eight rooms. She teaches Grade Five." My father shakes his head. "I can't think of her any way but when she was going to school, so shy I used to pick her up on the road – I'd be on my way to see you – and she would not say one word, not even to agree it was a nice day."

"She's got over that."

"Who are you talking about?" says the old lady.

"Muriel. I said she's got over being shy."

"She was here last summer."

"No Momma that was Isabel. Isabel and her family were here last summer. Muriel's out west."

"I meant Isabel."

Shortly after this the old lady falls asleep, her head on the side, her mouth open. "Excuse her manners," Nora says. "It's old age." She fixes an afghan over her mother and says we can all go into the front room where our talking won't disturb her.

"You two," my father says. "Do you want to go outside and amuse yourselves?"

Amuse ourselves how? Anyway I want to stay. The front room is more interesting than the kitchen, though barer. There is a gramophone and a pump organ and a picture on the wall of Mary, Jesus' mother – I know that much – in shades of bright blue and pink with a spiked band of light around her head. I know that such pictures are found only in the homes of Roman Catholics and so Nora must be one. We have never known any

Roman Catholics at all well, never well enough to visit in their houses. I think of what my grandmother and my Aunt Tena, over in Dungannon, used to always say to indicate that somebody was a Catholic. *So-and-so digs with the wrong foot,* they would say. *She digs with the wrong foot.* That was what they would say about Nora.

Nora takes a bottle, half full, out of the top of the organ and pours some of what is in it into the two glasses that she and my father have emptied of the orange drink.

"Keep it in case of sickness?" my father says.

"Not on your life," says Nora. "I'm never sick. I just keep it because I keep it. One bottle does me a fair time, though, because I don't care for drinking alone. Here's luck!" She and my father drink and I know what it is. Whisky. One of the things my mother has told me in our talks together is that my father never drinks whisky. But I see he does. He drinks whisky and he talks of people whose names I have never heard before. But after a while he turns to a familiar incident. He tells about the chamber-pot that was emptied out the window. "Picture me there," he says, "hollering my heartiest. *Oh, lady, it's your Walker Brothers man, anybody home?*" He does himself hollering, grinning absurdly, waiting, looking up in pleased expectation and then – oh, ducking, covering his head with his arms, looking as if he begged for mercy (when he never did anything like that, I was watching), and Nora laughs, almost as hard as my brother did at the time.

"That isn't true! That's not a word true!"

"Oh, indeed it is ma'am. We have our heroes in the ranks of Walker Brothers. I'm glad you think it's funny," he says sombrely.

I ask him shyly, "Sing the song."

"What song? Have you turned into a singer on top of everything else?"

Embarrassed, my father says, "Oh, just this song I made up while I was driving around, it gives me something to do, making up rhymes."

But after some urging he does sing it, looking at Nora with a droll, apologetic expression, and she laughs so much that in places he has to stop and wait for her to get over laughing so he can go on, because she makes him laugh too. Then he does various parts of his salesman's spiel. Nora when she laughs squeezes her large bosom under her folded arms. "You're crazy," she says. "That's all you are." She sees my brother peering into the gramophone and she jumps up and goes over to him. "Here's us sitting enjoying ourselves and not giving you a thought, isn't it terrible?" she says. "You want me to put a record on, don't you? You want to hear a nice record? Can you dance? I bet your sister can, can't she?"

I say no. "A big girl like you and so good-looking and can't dance!" says Nora. "It's high time you learned. I bet you'd make a lovely dancer. Here, I'm going to put on a piece I used to dance to and even your daddy did, in his dancing days. You didn't know your daddy was a dancer, did you? Well, he is a talented man, your daddy!"

She puts down the lid and takes hold of me unexpectedly around the waist, picks up my other hand and starts making me go backwards. "This is the way, now, this is how they dance. Follow me. This foot, see. One and one-two. One and one-two. That's fine, that's lovely, don't look at your feet! Follow me, that's right, see how easy? You're going to be a lovely dancer! One and one-two. One and one-two. Ben, see your daughter dancing!" *Whispering while you cuddle near me. Whispering where no one can hear me....*

Round and round the linoleum, me proud, intent, Nora laughing and moving with great buoyancy, wrapping me in her strange gaiety, her smell of whisky, cologne, and sweat. Under the arms her dress is damp, and little drops form along her upper lip, hang in the soft black hairs at the corners of her mouth. She whirls me around in front of my father – causing me to stumble, for I am by no means so swift a pupil as she pretends – and lets me go, breathless.

"Dance with me, Ben."

"I'm the world's worst dancer, Nora, and you know it."

"I certainly never thought so."

"You would now."

She stands in front of him, arms hanging loose and hopeful, her breasts, which a moment ago embarrassed me with their warmth and bulk, rising and falling under her loose flowered dress, her face shining with the exercise, and delight.

"Ben."

My father drops his head and says quietly, "Not me, Nora."

So she can only go and take the record off. "I can drink alone but I can't dance alone," she says. "Unless I am a whole lot crazier than I think I am."

"Nora," says my father smiling. "You're not crazy."

"Stay for supper."

"Oh, no. We couldn't put you to the trouble."

"It's no trouble. I'd be glad of it."

"And their mother would worry. She'd think I'd turned us over in a ditch."

"Oh, well. Yes."

"We've taken a lot of your time now."

"Time," says Nora bitterly. "Will you come by ever again?"

"I will if I can," says my father.

"Bring the children. Bring your wife."

"Yes I will," says my father. "I will if I can."

When she follows us to the car he says, "You come to see us too, Nora. We're right on Grove Street, left-hand side going in, that's north, and two doors this side – east – of Baker Street."

Nora does not repeat these directions. She stands close to the car in her soft, brilliant dress. She touches the fender, making an unintelligible mark in the dust there.

ON THE WAY HOME father does not buy any ice cream or pop, but he does go into a country store and get a package of licorice, which he shares with us. *She digs with the wrong foot,* I think, and the words seem sad to me as never before, dark, perverse. My father does not say anything to me about not mentioning things at home, but I know, just from the thoughtfulness, the pause when he passes the licorice, that there are things not to be mentioned. The whisky, maybe the dancing. No worry about my brother, he does not notice enough. At most he might remember the blind lady, the picture of Mary.

"Sing," my brother commands my father, but my father says gravely, "I don't know, I seem to be fresh out of songs. You watch the road and let me know if you see any rabbits."

So my father drives and my brother watches the road for rabbits and I feel my father's life flowing back from our car in the last of the afternoon, darkening and turning strange, like a landscape that has an enchantment on it, making it kindly, ordinary and familar while you are looking at it, but changing it, once your back is turned, into something you will never know, with all kinds of weathers, and distances you cannot imagine.

When we get closer to Tuppertown the sky becomes gently overcast, as always, nearly always, on summer evenings by the Lake.

[1968]

JOY WILLIAMS

Health

PAMMY IS IN AN UNPLEASANT Texas city, the city where she was born, in the month of her twelfth birthday. It is cold and cloudy. Soon it will rain. The rain will wash the film of ash off the car she is travelling in, volcanic ash that has drifted across the Gulf of Mexico, all the way from the Yucatan. Pammy is a stocky grey-eyed blonde, a daughter, travelling in her father's car, being taken to her tanning lesson.

This is her father's joke. She is being taken to a tanning session, twenty-five minutes long. She had requested this for her birthday, ten tanning sessions in a health spa. She had also asked for and received new wheels for her skates. They are purple Rannalli's. She had dyed her stoppers to match although the match was not perfect. The stoppers were a duller, cruder purple. Pammy wants to be a speed skater but she worries that she doesn't have the personality for it. "You've gotta have gravel in your gut to be in speed," her coach said. Pammy has mastered the duck walk but still doesn't have a good, smooth cross-over, and sometimes she fears that she never will.

Pammy and her father, Morris, are following a truck which is carrying a jumble of television sets. There is a twenty-four-inch console facing them on the open tailgate, restrained by rope, with a bullet hole in the exact center of the screen.

Morris drinks coffee from a plastic-lidded cup that fits into a bracket mounted just beneath the car's radio. Pammy has a friend, Wanda, whose stepfather has the same kind of plastic cup in his car, but he drinks bourbon and water from his. Wanda had been adopted when she was two months old. Pammy is relieved that neither her father nor Marge, her mother, drinks. Sometimes they have wine. On her birthday, even Pammy had wine with dinner. Marge and Morris seldom quarrel and she is grateful for this. This morning, however, she had seen them quarrel. Once again, her mother had borrowed her father's hairbrush and left long, brown hairs in it. Her father had taken the brush and cleaned it with a comb over the clean kitchen sink. Her father had left a nest of brown hair in the white sink.

In the car, the radio is playing a song called *Tainted Love*, a song Morris likes to refer to as *Rancid Love*. The radio plays constantly when Pammy and her father drive anywhere. Morris is a good driver. He is fast and doesn't bear grudges. He enjoys driving still, after years and years of it. Pammy looks forward to learning how to drive now, but after a few years, who knows? She can't imagine it being that enjoyable after a while. Her father is skillful here, on the freeways and streets, and on the terrifying, wide two-lane highways and narrow mountain roads in Mexico, and even on the rutted, soiled beaches of the Gulf Coast. One weekend, earlier that spring, Morris had rented a Jeep in Corpus Christi and he and Pammy and Marge had driven the length of Padre Island. They sped across the sand, the only people for miles and miles. There was plastic everywhere.

"You will see a lot of plastic," the man who rented them the Jeep said, "but it is plastic from all over the world."

Morris had given Pammy a lesson in driving the Jeep. He taught her how to shift smoothly, how to synchronize acceleration with the depression and release of the clutch. "There's a way to do things right," Morris told her and when he said this she was filled with a sort of fear. They were just words, she knew, words that anybody could use, but behind words were always things, sometimes things you could never tell anyone, certainly no one you loved, frightening things that weren't even true.

"I'm sick of being behind this truck," Morris says. The screen of the injured television looks like dirty water. Morris pulls to the curb beside an Oriental market. Pammy stares into the market where shoppers wait in line at a cash register. Many of the women wear scarves on their heads. Pammy is deeply disturbed by Orientals who kill penguins to make gloves and murder whales to make nail polish. In school, in social studies class, she is reading eyewitness accounts of the aftermath of the atomic bombing of Hiroshima. She reads about young girls running from their melting city, their hair burnt off, their burnt skin in loose folds, crying, "Stupid Americans." Morris sips his coffee, then turns the car back onto the street, a street now free from fatally wounded television sets.

Pammy gazes at the backs of her hands which are tan, but, she feels, not tan enough. They are a dusky peach color. This will be her fifth tanning lesson. In the health spa, there are ten colored photographs on the wall showing a woman in a bikini, a pale woman being transformed into a tanned woman. In the last photograph she has plucked the bikini slightly away from her hip-bone to expose a sliver of white skin and she is smiling down at the sliver.

Pammy tans well. Without a tan, her face seems grainy and uneven for she has freckles and rather large pores. Tanning draws her together, completes her. She has had all kinds of tans – golden tans, pool tans, even a Florida tan which seemed yellow back in Texas. She had brought all her friends the same present from Florida – small plywood crates filled with tiny oranges which were actually chewing gum. The finest tan Pammy has ever had, however, was in Mexico six months ago. She had gone there with her parents for two weeks, and she had gotten a truly remarkable tan and she had gotten tuberculosis. This has caused some tension between Morris and Marge as it had been Morris' idea to swim at the spas in the mountains rather than in the pools at the more established hotels. It was believed that Pammy had become infected at one particular public spa just outside the small dusty town where they had gone to buy tiles, tiles of a dusky orange with blue rays flowing from the center, tiles which are now in the kitchen of their home where each morning Pammy drinks her juice and takes three hundred milligrams of isoniazid.

"Here we are," Morris says. The health spa is in a small, concrete block building with white columns, salvaged from the wrecking of a mansion, adorning the front. There are gift shops, palmists and all-night restaurants along the street, as well as an exterminating company that has a huge fiberglass bug with Xs for eyes on the roof. This was not the company that had tented Wanda's house for termites. That had been another company. When Pammy was in Mexico getting tuberculosis, Wanda and her parents had gone to San Antonio for a week while their house was being tented. When they returned, they'd found a dead robber in the living room, the things he was stealing piled neatly nearby. He had died from inhaling the deadly gas used by the exterminators.

"Mommy will pick you up," Morris says. "She has a class this afternoon so she might be a little late. Just stay inside until she comes."

Morris kisses her on the cheek. He treats her like a child. He treats Marge like a mother, her mother.

Marge is thirty-five but she is still a student. She takes courses in art history and film at one of the city's universities, the same university where Morris teaches petroleum science. Years ago when Marge had first been a student, before she had met Morris and Pammy had been born, she had been in Spain, in a museum studying a Goya and a piece of the painting had fallen at her feet. She had quickly placed it in her pocket and now has it on her bureau in a small glass box. It is a wedge of greenish-violet paint, as large as a thumb-nail. It is from one of Goya's nudes.

Pammy gets out of the car and goes into the health spa. There is no equipment here except for the tanning beds, twelve tanning beds in eight small rooms. Pammy has never had to share a room with anyone. If asked to, she would probably say no, hoping that she would not hurt the other person's feelings. The receptionist is an old, vigorous woman behind a scratched metal desk, wearing a black jumpsuit and feather earrings. Behind her are shelves of powders and pills in squat brown bottles with names like DYNAMIC STAMINA BUILDER and DYNAMIC SUPER STRESS – END and LIVER CONCENTRATE ENERGIZER.

The receptionist's name is Aurora. Pammy thinks that the name is magnificent and is surprised that it belongs to such an old woman. Aurora leads her to one of the rooms at the rear of the building. The room has a mirror, a sink, a small stool, a white rotating fan and the bed, a long bronze coffin-like apparatus with a lid. Pammy is always startled when she sees the bed with its frosted ultraviolet tubes, its black vinyl headrest. In the next room, someone coughs. Pammy imagines people lying in all the rooms, wrapped in white light, lying quietly as though they were being rested for a long, long journey. Aurora takes a spray bottle of disinfectant and a scrap of toweling from the counter above the sink and cleans the surface of the bed. She twists the timer and the light leaps out, like an animal in a dream, like a murderer in a movie.

"There you are, honey," Aurora says. She pats Pammy on the shoulder and leaves.

Pammy pushes off her sandals and undresses quickly. She leaves her clothes in a heap, her sweatshirt on top of the pile. Her sweatshirt is white with a transfer of a skater on the back. The skater is a man wearing a helmet and knee-pads, side-surfing goofy-footed. She lies down and with her left hand pulls the lid to within a foot of the bed's cool surface. She can see the closed door and the heap of clothing and her feet. Pammy considers her feet to be her ugliest feature. They are skinny and the toes are too far apart. She and Wanda had painted their toes the same color, but Wanda's feet were pretty and hers were not. Pammy thought her feet looked like they belonged to a dead person and there wasn't anything she could do about them. She closes her eyes.

Wanda, who read a lot, told Pammy that tuberculosis was a very romantic disease, the disease of artists and poets and "highly sensitive individuals."

"Oh yeah," her stepfather had said. "Tuberculosis has mucho cachet."

Wanda's stepfather speaks loudly and his eyes glitter. He is always joking, Pammy thinks. Pammy feels that Wanda's parents are pleasant but she is always a little uncomfortable around them. They had a puppy for a while, a purebred Doberman which they gave to the SPCA after they discovered it had a slightly over-shot jaw. Wanda's stepfather always called the puppy a sissy. "You sissy," he'd say to the puppy. "Hanging around with girls all the time." He was referring to his wife and to Wanda and Pammy. "Oh, you sissy, you sissy," he'd say to the puppy.

There was also the circumstance of Wanda's adoption. There had been another baby adopted, but it was learned that the baby's background had been misrepresented. Or perhaps it had been a boring baby. In any case the baby had been returned and they got Wanda.

Pammy doesn't think Wanda's parents are very steadfast. She is surprised that they don't make Wanda nervous, for Wanda is certainly not perfect. She's a shoplifter and gets Cs in Computer Language.

The tanning bed is warm but not uncomfortably so. Pammy lies with her arms straight by her sides, palms down. She hears voices in the hall and footsteps. When she first began coming to the health spa, she was afraid that someone would open the door to the room she was in by mistake. She imagined exactly what it would be like. She would see the door open abruptly out of the corner of her eye, then someone would say, "Sorry," and the door would close again. But this had not happened. The voices pass by.

Pammy thinks of Snow White lying in her glass coffin. The Queen had deceived her how many times? Three? She had been in disguise, but still. And then Snow White had choked on an apple. In the restaurants she sometimes goes to with her parents there are posters on the walls which show a person choking and another person trying to save him. The posters take away Pammy's appetite.

Snow White lay in a glass coffin, not naked of course but in a gown, watched over by dwarfs. But surely they had not been real dwarfs. That had just been a word that had been given to them.

When Pammy had told Morris that tuberculosis was a romantic disease, he had said, "There's nothing romantic about it. Besides, you don't have it."

It seems to be a fact that she both has and doesn't have tuberculosis. Pammy had been given the tuberculin skin test along with her classmates when she began school in the fall and within forty-eight hours had a large swelling on her arm.

"Now that you've come in contact with it, you don't have to worry about getting it," the pediatrician had said in his office, smiling.

"You mean the infection constitutes immunity," Marge said.

"Not exactly," the pediatrician said, shaking his head, still smiling.

Her lungs are clear. She is not ill but has an illness. The germs are in her body, but in a resting state, still alive but rendered powerless, successfully overcome by her healthy body's strong defenses. Outwardly, she is the same, but within, a great drama had taken place and Pammy feels herself in possession of a bright, secret, and unspeakable knowledge.

She knows other things too, things that would break her parents' hearts, common, ugly, easy things. She knows a girl in school who stole her mother's green stamps and bought a personal massager with the books. She knows another girl whose brother likes to wear her clothes. She knows a boy who threw a can of motor oil at his father and knocked him unconscious.

Pammy stretches. Her head tingles. Her body is about a foot and a half off the floor and appears almost gray in the glare from the tubes. She has heard of pills one could take to acquire a tan. One just took two pills a day and after twenty days one had a wonderful tan which could be maintained just by taking two pills a day thereafter. You ordered them from Canada. It was some kind of food-coloring substance. How gross, Pammy thinks. When she had been little she had bought a quarter of an acre of land in Canada by mail for fifty cents. That had been two years ago.

Pammy hears voices from the room next to hers, coming through the thin wall. A woman talking rapidly says, "Pete went up to Detroit two days ago to visit his brother who's dying up there in the hospital. Cancer. The brother's always been a nasty type, I mean very unpleasant. Younger than Pete and always mean. Tried to commit suicide twice. Then he learns he has cancer and decides he doesn't want to die. Carries on and on. Is miserable to everyone. Puts the whole family through hell, but nothing can be done about it, he's dying of cancer. So Pete goes up to see him his last days in the hospital and you know what happens? Pete's wallet gets stolen. Right out of a dying man's room. Five hundred dollars in cash and all our credit cards. That was yesterday. What a day."

Another woman says, "If it's not one thing, it's something else."

Pammy coughs. She doesn't want to hear other people's voices. It is as though they are throwing away junk, the way some people use words, as though one word were as good as another.

"Things happen so abruptly any more," the woman says. "You know what I mean?"

Pammy does not listen and she does not open her eyes for if she did she would see this odd bright room with her clothes in a heap and herself lying motionless and naked. She does not open her eyes because she prefers imagining that she is a magician's accomplice, levitating on a stage in a coil of pure energy. If one thought purely enough, one could create one's own truth. That's how people accomplished astral travel, walked over burning coals, cured warts. There was a girl in Pammy's class at school, Bonnie Black, a small owlish looking girl who was a Christian Scientist. She raised rabbits and showed them at fairs, and was always wearing the ribbons they had won to school, pinned to her blouse. She had warts all over her hands, but one day Pammy noticed that the warts were gone and Bonnie Black had told her that the warts disappeared after she had clearly realized that in her true being as God's reflection, she couldn't have warts.

It seemed that people were better off when they could concentrate on something, hold something in their mind for a long time and really believe it. Pammy had once seen a radical skater putting on a show at the opening of a shopping mall. He leapt over cars and pumped up the sides of buildings. He did flips and spins. A disc jockey who was set up for the day in the parking lot interviewed him. "I'm really impressed with your performance," the disc jockey said, "and I'm impressed that you never fall. Why don't you fall?" The skater was a thin boy in baggy cut-off jeans. "I don't fall," the boy said, looking hard at the microphone, "because I've got a deep respect for the concrete surface and because when I make a miscalculation, instead of falling, I turn it into a new trick."

Pammy thinks it is wonderful that the boy was able to say something which would keep him from thinking he might fall.

The door to the room opened. Pammy had heard the turning of the knob. At first she lies without opening her eyes, willing the sound of the door shutting, but she hears nothing, only the ticking of the bed's timer. She swings her head quickly to the side and looks at the door. There is a man standing there, staring at her. She presses her right hand into a fist and lays it between her legs. She puts her left arm across her breasts.

"What?" she says to the figure, frightened. In an instant she is almost panting with fear. She feels the repetition of something painful and known, but she has not known this, not ever. The figure says nothing and pulls the door shut. With a flurry of rapid ticking, the timer stops. The harsh lights of the bed go out.

Pammy pushes the lid back and hurriedly gets up. She dresses hastily and smooths her hair with her fingers. She looks at herself in the mirror, her lips parted. Her teeth are white behind her pale lips. She stares at herself. She can be looked at and not discovered. She can speak and not be known. She opens the door and enters the hall. There is no one there. The hall is so narrow that by spreading her arms she can touch the walls with her fingertips. In the reception area by Aurora's desk, there are three people, a stoop-shouldered young woman and two men. The woman was signing up for a month of unlimited tanning which meant that after the basic monthly fee she only had to pay a dollar a visit. She takes her checkbook out of a soiled handbag, which is made out of some silvery material, and writes a check. The men look comfortable lounging in the chairs, their legs stretched out. They know one another, Pammy guesses, but they do not know the woman. One of them has dark spikey hair like a wet animal's. The other wears a red tight T-shirt. Neither is the man she had seen in the doorway.

"What time do you want to come back tomorrow, honey?" Aurora asks Pammy. "You certainly are coming along nicely. Isn't she coming along nicely?"

"I'd like to come back the same time tomorrow," Pammy says. She raises her hand to her mouth and coughs slightly.

"Not the same time, honey. Can't give you the same time. How about an hour later?"

"All right," Pammy says. The stoop-shouldered woman sits down in a chair. There are no more chairs in the room. Pammy opens the door to the street and steps outside. It has rained and the street is dark and shining. The air smells fresh and feels thick. She stands in it, a little stunned, looking. Her father will teach her how to drive, and she will drive around. Her mother will continue to take classes at the university. Whenever she meets someone new, she will mention the Goya. "I have a small Goya," she will say, and laugh.

Pammy walks slowly down the street. She smells barbecued meat and the rain lingering in the trees. By a store called IMAGINE, there's a clump of bamboo with some beer cans glittering in its ragged, grassy center. IMAGINE sells neon palm trees and silk clouds and stars. It sells greeting cards and chocolate in shapes children aren't allowed to see and it sells children stickers and shoelaces. Pammy looks in the window at a huge satin pillow in the shape of a heart with a heavy zipper running down the center of it. Pammy turns and walks back to the building that houses the tanning beds. Her mother pulls up in the car. "Pammy!" she calls. She is leaning toward the window on the passenger side which she has rolled down. She unlocks the car's door. Pammy gets in and the door locks again.

Pammy wishes she could tell her mother something, but what can she say? She never wants to see that figure looking at her again, so coldly staring and silent, but she knows she will, for already its features are becoming more indistinct, more general. It could be anything. She coughs, but it is not the cough of a sick person because Pammy is a healthy girl. It is the kind of cough a person might make if they were at a party and there was no one there but strangers.

Marge, driving, says, "You look very nice. That's a very pretty tan, but what will happen when you stop going there? It won't last. You'll lose it right away, won't you?"

She will. And she will grow older, but the world will remain as young as she was once, infinite in its possibilities and uncaring.

ALICE ADAMS

The Oasis

IN PALM SPRINGS the poor are as dry as old brown leaves, blown in from the desert – wispily thin and almost invisible. Perhaps they are embarrassed at finding themselves among so much opulence (indeed, why are they there at all? why not somewhere else?), among such soaring, thick-trunked palms, such gleamingly white, palatial hotels.

And actually, poor people are only seen in the more or less outlying areas, the stretch of North Canyon Drive, for example, where even the stores are full of sleazy, cut-rate goods, and the pastel stucco hotels are small, one-story, and a little seedy, with small, shallow, too-bright blue pools. The poor are not seen in those stores, though, and certainly not in even the tawdriest motels; they stick to the street; for the most part they keep moving. A hunched-up, rag-bound man with his swollen bundle (of what? impossible to guess) might lean against a sturdy palm tree, so much fatter and stronger than he is – but only for a moment, and he would be looking around, aware of himself as displaced. And on one of the city benches a poor woman with her plastic splintered bag looks perched there, an uneasy, watchful bird, with sharp, fierce, wary eyes.

A visibly rich person would look quite odd there too, in that nebulous, interim area, unless he or she were just hurrying through – maybe running, in smart pale jogging clothes, or briskly stepping along toward the new decorator showrooms, just springing up on the outskirts of town. In any case, rich people, except in cars, are seen in that particular area of Palm Springs quite as infrequently as the very poor are.

However, on a strange day in early April – so cold, such a biting wind, in a place where bad weather is almost unheard of and could be illegal – on that day a woman all wrapped in fine pale Italian wool and French silk, with fine, perfect champagne hair and an expensive color on her mouth – that woman, whose name is Clara Gibson, sits on a bench in what she knows is the wrong part of Palm Springs (she also knows that it is the wrong day for her to be there), and she wonders what on earth to do.

There are certain huge and quite insoluble problems lying always heavily on her mind (is this true of everyone? She half suspects that it is, but has wondered); these have to do with her husband and her daughter, and with an entity that she vaguely and rather sadly thinks of as herself. But at the moment she can do nothing about any of these three quite problematic people. And so she concentrates on what is immediate, the fact that she has a billfold full of credit cards and almost no cash: a ten, two ones, not even much change. And her cards are not coded for sidewalk cash withdrawal from banks because her husband, Bradley, believes that this is dangerous. Also: today is Tuesday, and because she confused the dates (or something) she will be here alone until Thursday, when Bradley arrives. The confusion itself is suspicious, so unlike her; was she anxious to get away from her daughter, Jennifer, whom she was just visiting in San Francisco? Or, did she wish to curtail Bradley's time alone at his meetings, in Chicago? However, this is not the time for such imponderables. She must simply decide what to do for the rest of the afternoon, and where best to go for dinner – by herself, on a credit card; the hotel in which she is staying (the wrong hotel, another error) does not serve meals.

And she must decide whether or not to give her last ten dollars to the withered, dessicated woman, with such crazed, dark, terrified eyes, whom she has been watching on the bench one down from hers. A woman very possibly her own age, or maybe younger; no one could tell. But: should she give her the money, and if so how? (It hardly matters whether Clara is left with ten or two.)

And: why has this poor woman come to Palm Springs, of all places? Was it by mistake? Is she poor because a long time ago she made a mistaken, wrong marriage – just as Clara's own was so eminently "right"? (Marriage, for women, has often struck Clara as a sort of horse race.) But now Clara passionately wonders all these things about this woman, and she wonders too if there is a shelter for such people here. From time to time she has given money to some of the various shelter organizations in New York, where she comes from, but she has meant to do more, perhaps to go and work in one. Is there a welfare office with emergency funds available for distribution? Or have all the cuts that one reads about affected everything? Lots of MX missiles, no relief. Is there a free clinic, in case the woman is sick?

Something purple is wound among the other garments around that woman's shoulders: a remnant of a somewhat better life or a handout from someone? But it can't be warm, that purple thing, and the wind is terrible.

If Clara doesn't somehow – soon – give her the money, that woman will be gone, gone scuttering down the street like blown tumbleweed, thinks Clara, who is suddenly sensing the desert that surrounds them as an inimical force. Miles of desert, which she has never seen before, so much vaster than this small, square, green, artificial city.

CLARA'S PLANE had arrived promptly at 10:10 this morning, and after her first strange views of gray, crevassed mountains, the airport building was comfortingly small, air-conditioned (unnecessary, as things turned out, in this odd cold weather), with everything near and accessible.

The first thing she found out was that the plane from Chicago, due in at 10:30 (this reunion has been a masterpiece of timing, Clara had thought) would not arrive until 11:04. An easy wait;

Clara even welcomed the time, during which she could redo her face (Brad, a surgeon, is a perfectionist in such matters), and reassemble her thoughts about and reactions to their daughter. What to tell Brad and what to relegate to her own private, silent scrutiny.

Should it be upsetting that a daughter in her early thirties earns more money than her father does at almost twice her age, her father the successful surgeon? (Clara has even secretly thought that surgeons quite possibly charge too much: is it right, really, for operations to impoverish people? not to mention rumors that some operations are not even necessary?) In any case, Jennifer, a corporation lawyer, is a very rich, very young person. And she is unhappy, and the cause of her discomfort is nothing as simple as not being married – the supposedly classic complaint among young women of her age. Jennifer does not want to get married, yet, although she goes out a great deal with young men. What she seems to want, really, is even more money than she has, and more *things*. She has friends of her own age and education who are earning more money than she is, even, who own more boats and condominiums. This is all very distressing to her mother; the very unfamiliarity of such problems and attitudes is upsetting (plus the hated word Yuppie, which would seem to apply). Resolutely, as she sat there in the waiting room, Clara, with her perfectly made up face, decided that she would simply say to Brad, "Well, Jennifer's fine. She looks marvelous, she's going out a lot but nothing serious. And she's earning scads of money." (Scads? A word she has not used nor surely heard for many years, not since the days when she seemed to understand so much more than she seems to now.)

Brad, though, was not among the passengers from Chicago who poured through the gate in their inappropriate warm-weather vacation clothes, swinging tennis rackets, sacks of golf clubs.

Clara sat down to think. Out of habit, then, and out of some small nagging suspicion, she checked her small pocket notebook – and indeed it was she who had arrived on the wrong day,

Tuesday. Brad would come, presumably, on Thursday.

Just next to her yellow plastic bench was a glassed-in gift shop where she could see a shelf of toy animals, one of which she remarked on as especially appealing: a silky brown dog about the size of some miniature breed. Now, as Clara watched, a woman in a fancy pink pants suit came up to exclaim, to stroke the head of the toy. A man, her companion, did the same, and then another group came over to pet and to exclaim over the adorable small false dog.

Clara found this small tableau unaccountably disturbing, and on a sudden wave of decisiveness she got up and went out to the curb where the taxis and hotel limousines assembled. She asked the snappily uniformed man about transportation to the Maxwell. Oh yes, he assured her; a limousine. And then, "You know there're two Maxwells?"

No, Clara did not know that.

His agile eyes appraised her hair, her careful face, her clothes. "Well, I'm sure you'd be going to the Maxwell Plaza," he concluded, and he ushered her into a long white stretch Mercedes, in which she was driven for several miles of broad palm-lined streets to a huge but wonderfully low-key hotel, sand-colored – the desert motif continued in cactus plantings, a green display of succulents.

At the desk, though, in that largest and most subdued of lobbies, Clara was gently, firmly informed that she (they) had no reservation. And, "Could Mrs. Gibson just possibly have booked into the Maxwell Oasis by mistake?" This of course was the Maxwell *Plaza*.

Well, indeed it was possible that Clara had made that mistake. However, should anyone, especially her husband, *Doctor* Gibson, call or otherwise try to get in touch with her here, at the Plaza, would they kindly direct him to the Oasis, which is (probably) where Clara would be?

The Maxwell Oasis is out on North Canyon Drive, not far from the bench on which Clara was to sit and to observe the windblown man and the fierce-eyed, purple-swathed bag lady.

The Oasis is small, a pink-stucco, peeling, one-story building, with a small blue oblong pool. All shrouded with seedy bougainvillea. And it was there, indeed, that Clara by some chance or mischance had made a reservation. But for Thursday, not Tuesday, not today; however, luckily, they still had a room available.

IN THE LOWER LEVEL bar of the Maxwell Plaza, though, the desert has been lavishly romanticized: behind the huge, deep, dark leather armchairs are glassed-in displays of permanently flowering cactus, interesting brown shapes of rocks, and bright polished skulls (not too many skulls, just a tasteful few).

Clara, after her meditative, observant afternoon on the bench, decided that it would make some sort of sense to come to this hotel for a drink and dinner. But just now (so out of character for her) she is engaged in telling a series of quite egregious lies to some people who are perfectly all right, probably, but who have insisted that she join them for a drink. A couple: just plain rich, aging people from Seattle, who assume that a woman alone must be lonely.

"Of course I've always loved the desert," has been Clara's first lie. The desert on closer acquaintance could become acutely terrifying is what she truly thinks.

She has also given them a curious version of her daughter, Jennifer, describing her as a social worker in East Oakland, "–not much money but she's *very* happy." And she has been gratified to hear her companions, "Oh, isn't that nice! So many young people these days are so – so materialistic. What is it they call them? Yuppies!" Beaming at Clara, who is not the mother of a Yuppie.

The only excuse that Clara can make for her own preposterousness is that their joining her was almost forcible. She was enjoying her drink alone and her private thoughts. She was recalling what happened earlier that very afternoon, when, just as she was reaching into her purse for the ten-dollar bill which, yes, she would give to the bag lady (who fortunately seemed to have dozed off on her bench) Clara remembered the hundred secreted (always, on Brad's instructions) in the lining of her bag. And so, tiptoeing (feeling foolish, tiptoes on a sidewalk) Clara slipped both bills down into the red plastic bag, out of sight.

She had been imagining, thinking of the woman's discovery of the money – surely she would be pleased? She needed it for something? – at the very moment these Seattle tourists came and practically sat on top of her.

Clara has also been thinking of how Brad would have objected. But what will that woman do with it, he would have wondered. Suppose she has a drinking problem? Clara recognizes that she herself does not much care what the woman does with her money; she simply wanted to make the gift of it. It will do no harm, she believes – although pitifully little good, so little to assuage the thick, heavy terribleness of that life, of most lives.

And then she heard, "Well, you can't sit there drinking all by yourself? You must let us join you."

Aside from their ill-timed intrusiveness, these people are annoying to Clara because (she has to face this) in certain clear ways they so strongly resemble herself and Brad. The woman's hair is the same improbably fragile pale wine color, her clothes Italian/French. And the man's clothes are just like Brad's, doctor-banker-lawyer clothes (Nixon-Reagan clothes). The couple effect is markedly similar.

And so, partly to differentiate herself from these honest, upright, upper-middle class citizens, Clara continues to lie.

"No, my husband isn't coming along on this trip," she tells them. "I like to get away by myself." And she smiles, a bright, independent-woman smile. "My life in New York seems impossible sometimes."

As she thinks, Well, that is at least partially true. And, conceivably, Brad too has confused the dates, and will not show up for some time – another week? I could be here by myself for quite a while, Clara thinks, though she knows this to be unlikely. But I could go somewhere else?

No, she says to the couple from Seattle, she is not going to have dinner in this hotel. She has to meet someone.

Actually Clara on the way here noticed a big, flashy delicatessen, a place that assuredly will take her credit cards. But, a place where a bag lady might possibly go? A bag lady with a little recent cash? Very likely not; still, the very possibility is more interesting than that of dinner with this couple.

Clara stands up, and the gentleman too rises. "Well," says Clara, "I've certainly enjoyed talking to you."

Which she very much hopes will be her last lie for quite some time, even if that will take a certain rearrangement of her life.

JANE BOWLES

Señorita Córdoba

ONE MORNING Señorita Córdoba received a letter from her mother. She sat beside the fountain reading it.

My Dear Violeta –

I do hope you are enjoying every minute of your stay in the city of Antigua. It is a great miracle to think that Antigua has been destroyed once by fire and once by water. My father pointed out the beauty of this city to me at an early age. He said to me, "When you go to Europe, you need not bow your head in shame that you have come from a country inhabited almost entirely by Indians, as many Europeans are wont to believe. But say to them proudly, "If Europe were a crown and in this crown one jewel were missing – the most beautiful jewel of all – you would find it in my country situated between two volcanoes and surrounded by hills. Its name is Antigua." At that age I loved to sit among the ruins, but Aunt Mercedes (who has come to agree with me), Aunt Mercedes and I still think it a little unwise for you to have taken such a trip at this particular moment. I realize it is only a few hours away, of course. Did you say that your board was fifty cents a day? For that they should serve you all the chicken you wanted and if they don't I hope you will be sure to demand your just rights. The lady of the pension will understand. I think perhaps that I as your mother have been a little too spiritual all my life. I do not want you to be the same. Perhaps, though, spiritual would not be the correct term to apply to you. Aunt Mercedes and I have been contenting ourselves with eggs and beans. The meat has been unusually hard this week and so very dear. I don't want you to worry about this or let it spoil your lovely holiday. You might try to buy a picture of the All Saints' Day parade from someone who has a camera. Try not to buy it – ask for it, nicely. Señora Sanchez was in the other evening. She was riding by on a horse and she stopped in. She was complaining bitterly about prices, and insulted me grossly, I thought, by handing me half a chicken enveloped in some newspaper, which I handed over to the servants, of course. Aunt Mercedes didn't think that was quite wise. She is a great chicken eater, while I myself am more or less indifferent to all foods, as you know. Aunt Mercedes thought it dreadful that she should be riding on a horse, so soon after her husband's death. We send you our best wishes for an agreeable holiday. May the Lord bless you and keep you well.

Your mother

Señorita Córdoba frowned and looked into the fountain. "Such an old-fashioned letter," she thought to herself. "My mother and my aunt are living like cliff dwellers. Such people write a letter about a chicken." She took a pencil from her bag and made some figures on a piece of paper. She knew just about how much money she needed to get back to Paris and to live there for a little while, while she was starting her dress establishment. She was going to make dresses with a Latin spirit. There was only one way for her to get hold of this money, she was certain, and that was through a man. She had seen a lot of this going on in Paris, and she thought that she would know how to handle such a situation if she could possibly meet a man rich enough in Guatemala. "It would all be in a first-class way," she had assured herself.

On the following morning Señorita Córdoba overheard Señora Ramirez telling the children that their father would arrive that day. She was delighted to hear this, because she knew Señor Ramirez to be one of the richest men in the country...and a great lady lover. It was on the chance that he would come to Antigua to visit his wife and children that she herself had decided to spend the Holy Week in Señora Espinoza's pension. She knew that Señora Ramirez had been spending the Semana Santa there now for many years, or so she had heard tell from her mother and her mother's friends, who had never understood why Señor

Ramirez did not send his wife to a more expensive touristic hotel. He had never been seen at the pension with her until the previous year, when he had suddenly appeared in Antigua and stayed there for several days. However, most people said that he had come to spend his time with his friend Alfonso Gutierres, who had opened an unfrequented but very elegant hotel which was reputed to have the best wine cellar and hard liquor stock in the country. Señorita Córdoba, having heard of his former visit, had been very much in hopes that he would return again this season. She had thought the short journey well worth the risk, particularly as she was tired of helping her mother with the coffee finca and the house – two things which interested her less than anything in the world. She was delighted that he was arriving so promptly. She was never able to relax or enjoy anything that was not concerned directly with the making of her life. Now she was in a feverish state, pulling her dresses out of her trunk and examining them for holes. The figure that she had decided was the minimum sum which she would demand for her trip and to cover the initial investment in her dress shop, and of course her first six months living in Paris, she had marked down on a pad which lay on the bureau. She went over and looked at the pad now, and her cheeks were quite flushed with the intensity of her figuring. She stood there for a long time and then she changed the number on the pad. She made it a little lower.

She picked up a long silk ball dress that she had not worn for many years. It was pink, and to the bodice were pinned some shapeless silk flowers. She decided to wear this to dinner, as it was the fanciest thing she had and was certain to please a Spanish man. She lay down on the bed. Her face was strained and stiff. She shut her eyes for a moment and thought of the name of her shop. It was to be called "Casa Córdoba." "Now," she said to herself, "for what the French call beauty sleep. No thoughts – no thoughts – just rest." She could hear marimba music playing over the radio. She loved listening to music, and it made her think of all the things which she considered beautiful – Venice and the opera and the hall of mirrors in the palace at Versailles.

To her, luxury and beauty (beauty there was none without at least the luxury of past splendor) were synonymous with morality, and when people lived well she considered them to be good people and when they lived really luxuriously she considered them to be saints. The marimba music and her memory of Venice and her walk through the hall of mirrors gave her such a feeling of the goodness of God that she crossed herself and decided to buy a candle in the church after her siesta.

The diners had all taken their places when Señorita Córdoba entered the room. The Ramirez daughters, Consuela and Lilina, were seated on either side of their father, wearing their fiesta dresses. The servant stood in confusion before Señor Ramirez because he had ordered her not to bother with the soup but to bring him instead a large portion of meat and some beer right away.

"Wouldn't you like some soup first?" Maria asked him. Ramirez was beginning to lose his temper when he saw Señorita Córdoba enter the room. She had brightened her cheeks with some rouge, and on the whole she looked quite beautiful. Señor Ramirez's mouth hung open. He turned completely around in his chair and stared at Violeta. The traveler rose at the same time and rushed over to Señorita Córdoba as though he had never seen her before. She blushed a bright pink and her eyebrows twitched. To get away from all this attention she went over to the English lady in the corner and began to talk to her. The English lady was very much surprised because she had never received more than a curt nod from Miss Córdoba before this moment.

"Miss," said Violeta, "I wish you would take a walk with me some morning. I think it is a shame that we haven't become better acquainted with one another."

"Yes, it is, isn't it," answered the English lady. Miss Córdoba's armpits were wet with nervous sweat. She was terribly embarrassed since she had entered the room in her ball dress. She was bending over the English lady with one hand placed flat on the table, and she noticed that the English lady was looking into her bodice, a faint expression of disgust visible in her face, the disgust of an English person who does not like to be near a foreigner.

"You Spanish girls all have such beautiful olive skin," she said. This was a completely hysterical thing for her to say because Violeta's skin was whiter than her own. She continued, "I would be very glad to take a walk with you but I am sure you will still be in the arms of Morpheus when I have already eaten my breakfast and written my letters for the day. I can't walk after ten because the sun tires me so. I have as a matter of fact covered the ground here thoroughly but I am looking forward to the processions. A friend described them to me so beautifully that I've been longing to see them ever since. A wonderful gift, to make other people see things. I am more or less mute myself. I have been impressed by the colors here. What a sense of color the Indians have. They are famous for it, aren't they?"

"Oh yes, very famous. I will see you then soon?"

"Perhaps."

Señorita Córdoba had nothing to do but to go back to the table and submit to the stares of Señor Ramirez and the appraising glances of the traveler. Out of exuberance Señor Ramirez decided to focus his attention on his older, eleven-year-old child, Consuela.

"Now I think it would do you some good if you drank a big glass of beer," he said. "The Germans always give their children beer and look what a fine race of people they are."

"I don't want any beer, thank you, papa."

"You've never tried it so you don't know whether or not you like it." He poured her some beer and put it in front of her but she made no attempt to drink it. "You heard papa say that he wanted you to drink some beer."

"What kind of a crazy idea is this?" asked Señora Ramirez.

"What kind of a crazy girl is this that she won't drink beer?" answered Señor Ramirez.

"Yes, drink, Consuela," said Señora Ramirez. "What is the matter with you?" She pushed the glass up to her daughter's lips but Consuela refused to drink, although her mouth was covered with foam. The girl's eyes were beginning to shine. With a sudden jerking of her arm she knocked the glass out of her mother's hand, and the beer flowed over the table. Then she jumped up and down and screamed. Señorita Córdoba turned halfway around in her chair and looked at her bitterly. And partly for this reason, and partly because Consuela herself was in love with the traveler and certain that the traveler in turn loved Señorita Córdoba, Consuela lunged toward her and started to scratch Señorita Córdoba's face and to tear her coiffure apart. Violeta, with an icy smile on her face, stuck her leg out in order to trip Consuela, but in so doing she miscalculated and slid off her chair onto the floor. Consuela ran from the room, and both the traveler and Señor Ramirez helped Violeta up from the floor. She leaned her head on her hand and cried a little because the incident had so unnerved her. Señor Ramirez ordered a glass of beer for Señorita Córdoba.

"You drink that, Señorita," he said, "and when I am finished eating I will beat my daughter. I promise you that."

"I hope that you will," said Señorita Córdoba.

"Never before," said the English lady, "have I met three such horrid people. The daughter a real Fury, unable to control herself, the father a child-beater, and the young woman full of revenge, willing to have the child beaten. My digestion is spoiled." She threw her napkin onto the table and left the room.

"Who is that one?" Señor Ramirez asked his wife.

"A tourist who eats here every day."

"She takes everything hard," said the traveler, turning to Señorita Córdoba. "Single women of her age do, you know. In our country we call them old maids."

"What is the difference what she is," said Señorita Córdoba. "To me she is no more than a flea."

"That's right," said Señor Ramirez. "That's right. Most people are fleas – fleas with big stomachs but nothing in their heads."

"But those big stomachs have to be fed," said the traveler, thinking that this was going to be a political discussion. "Or do you believe in letting them eat cake?"

"Cake? I don't care what they eat." The traveler decided not to explain about Marie Antoinette. Señorita Córdoba had composed herself completely by now, and she turned to Señor Ramirez.

"I am Señorita Violeta Córdoba," she said to him, disregarding all traditions of ladylike behavior, for she had always been able to throw tradition to the four winds without being in the least revolutionary. "Thank you for having lifted me from the floor onto my seat."

"And what about me?" said the traveler. "Don't I count in this at all?" Señorita Córdoba nodded to him without smiling. Ramirez stood up and toasted Señorita Córdoba with his beer. "To a beautiful lady," he said, "as beautiful as a red rose." They were speaking together in English.

"A thousand thanks," said Señorita Córdoba quickly. "Let us hope that you mean what you say, and are not just a poet."

"I can be a poet when I want to be, but it is only one of twenty or thirty things that I can do."

SEÑOR GUTIERRES' HOTEL was austere but very elegant. The patio around which it was built was very small and almost always very dark. Looking down into it from the third floor, it was hard to distinguish the bushes and the few flower beds. Each bedroom was decorated in order to look as much like the bedroom of a Spanish king or nobleman as possible. The beds were on raised daises and the monogram of the hotel was on each pillow slip. The walls were rough and decorated with crossed sabres and blue or gold banners. The chairs were made of a very dark wood with carved narrow backs and little satin cushions tied to the seats by means of four tassels. Off the patio were two small dining rooms for those guests who preferred not to eat in the presence of strangers, and one large dining room that was public. In the public living room there was a veritable collection of sabres with fancy hilts, and chairs with backs that reached halfway up the wall. It was impossible to see in this room at all during the day, and at night the weak electric lamps left the corners of the room in total darkness.

Señor Gutierres was a gloomy businessman born in Spain who claimed to have noble blood. He was out in the back court, a place to which the guests had no access, wrangling with the cook about a chicken which he was holding by its feet and pinching. He was very thin and had deep circles under his eyes. There were a great many badly made rabbit hutches around, and a tremendous chicken coop. He was one of the few people in the country who kept his chickens in a coop. However, there were three large holes in the wiring and the chickens stepped in and out of the coop freely. The courtyard was a mess and it was just beginning to drizzle when Señor Ramirez came out and clapped his friend on the shoulder. "How about coming down to the bar and having a drink with me?" Señor Gutierres nodded and smiled for a second and together they went to the bar, which was underground and smelled very strongly of new wood. The bar stools were made of barrels. Señor Ramirez sat down on one of these and Señor Gutierres dropped the chicken, which he was still holding, onto the floor. The chicken began to strut around the shiny wooden floor, pecking at whatever it saw.

"How do you like my bar now that it is completed?"

"I will like your brandy even better when I have completed a bottle of that."

"Do you like my bar?" Señor Gutierres said again, determined to get an answer out of Señor Ramirez.

"Beautiful."

"I have designed the whole hotel for movie actresses and actors when they are on their vacations. They will be coming down over that highway like flies when it is finished." He looked at Señor Ramirez to see if he was of the same opinion, but his friend was staring hard at the labels on the bottles.

"A lot of people on their honeymoons, too. Rich people who like to go far, far away when they get married." He took down a bottle of brandy from the shelf and served himself and Señor Ramirez.

"You don't think much about this new highway. I dream about it by day and by night. You will see a difference in the hotels in this country when it is built. You won't recognize the place you were born in inside of five years. No?"

Señor Gutierres could never get it through his head that Norberto Ramirez was not interested in anything but having a good time and wielding a certain amount of power. He had inherited most of his money and was successful because he had the character of a bully. Señor Gutierres could not imagine that anyone as important and as impressive as Señor Ramirez should not be interested in business. He believed that his friend's disinclination to talk on any subject of interest was merely a ruse, which he had long ago decided to ignore.

"I have built my hotel purposely so soon because later it will not be so cheap. I have already quite a few guests who come here because they know they get good quality. They are all quality people. Everything has to be right for them. It is just as cheap to be right as to be wrong, my friend, you know that, and with a war coming in Europe, all these with quality who used to go to Biarritz will come here. And I am not going to make cheap prices for them. They mustn't pay anything different from what they were paying at Biarritz, otherwise they will say to themselves, Look, what is this? There is something wrong – so cheap, and they will even get to worry that there might be lower-class people in the same hotel. No, they must be taken like sleeping babies from one bed to another, quietly, so they don't wake up. A little Spanish decoration for a change will be all right. But if you notice this hotel is made to remind you more or less of a palace."

One of the Indian servants appeared in the doorway. She looked to be about forty and she was nursing a baby at her breast and smiling. "What do you want, Luz?" asked Señor Gutierres.

"I have come for the chicken, Señor. He must feel very sad for he is estranged from the other chickens, his brothers and his sisters, and the poor little thing cannot find anything to eat here." She started to chase it. The chicken spread its wings and ran as fast as it could around and around the room. The baby started to howl.

"Stop it, stop it!" shouted Señor Gutierres. "You can come and get him later."

"No, wait a minute, man," said Señor Ramirez, climbing down from his stool. "I will get this chicken." He spread his arms out and chased it from corner to corner, making terrible scratches in the wooden floor with the heels of his shoes, to the horror of Señor Gutierres, who began to rub his nose nervously with the back of his hand. Señor Ramirez was quite red in the face by now and beginning to lose his balance. He made a lunge toward the chicken and managed to corner it, but in so doing he fell sideways onto the floor and managed to crush the chicken beneath him.

"Ay," said the servant. "Now it is dead we shall have to cook it for tomorrow night's supper."

"Take it away, for the love of God," said Señor Gutierres, lifting his friend to his feet and handing the bloody chicken to the servant.

"What a shame, what a shame." The servant shook her head and left the room. They had another brandy together and did not bother to clean up the blood and the feathers which stuck both to one side of Señor Ramirez' coat and to the floor.

SEÑORITA CÓRDOBA meanwhile had had enough of waiting around the patio for the problematic return of Señor Ramirez. "My God," she said to herself, "I have no time to lose. I am behaving like a person with not a brain in her head." Besides, it had begun to rain and it was incredibly gloomy sitting there under the eaves, which projected a little bit from the house for the purpose of protecting one from the sun and from the rain. She went into her room, painted her face a bit more, and changed to a short dress. Then she decided to knock on Señora Ramirez' door and by some ruse try to find out where this lady's husband was likely to be. This she did and at first received no answer.

She knocked a little harder. "Come in," said Señora Ramirez in a voice that was caught in her throat. Señorita Córdoba opened the door and saw that Señora Ramirez and the two girls were lying on their beds, in a row. Consuela's dark eyes showed intense suffering as she rolled them slowly in the direction of the door. Lilina, seeing that it was Señorita Córdoba, pulled her pillow out from behind her head and buried her face beneath it. Señora Ramirez' eyes were swollen with sleep and she looked very much as though nothing would ever interest her again. Señorita Córdoba decided to ignore the mood that was in the room and she went hastily to the foot of Señora Ramirez' bed.

"I thought perhaps that you would be feeling rather badly as a result of this afternoon's events, and I came in to tell you more or less not to brood about it, and to ask you whether or not I could help you with anything."

Señora Ramirez nodded her head, and closed her eyes. Señorita Córdoba was growing impatient. She looked down at Consuela. "You, young girl," she said, "you should apologize to me." Consuela shook her head from side to side. "No," she said, "no, you are a very bad woman." She patted her heart.

"Well, Señora Ramirez, your daughter is a maniac. I am a religious woman and I am a very busy woman. That is all that anybody can say of me."

"Certainly," agreed Señora Ramirez, opening her eyes. "That is all anyone can say. And of me they can say that I am a mother of two children, and also a woman with a great many heartaches."

"I suppose you are wondering where your husband is at this very moment."

"No, no," said Señora Ramirez. "He is always outside somewhere."

Señorita Córdoba was exasperated. "But *where?* Where could he be?"

"With Gutierres, drinking."

"Who is Gutierres?"

"He is the owner of a hotel. It is called the Hotel Alhambra. My husband has never taken me to meet him and I shall probably never meet him before the day that I die."

Having gathered the information that she had been seeking, Señorita Córdoba hurriedly took her leave, warning Consuela at the door that she had better repent shortly. And then she was on her way, with an even and decided gait, like someone who has been sent on an important mission by the head of an organization. She was not a person who envisioned failure often, but only the interminable steps toward success.

When she arrived at the hotel she found a servant in the patio and inquired of her where she could find Señor Gutierres. "He is in the bar," said the servant, leading the way slowly.

"Good evening," said Señorita Córdoba, entering the room. "I hope that I have not interrupted a serious business conversation. Women have a very bad habit of doing this."

"Women have no bad habits," said Señor Ramirez, climbing down from his stool and taking her by the arm a little roughly.

"I got it into my head," said Señorita Córdoba, "that I would like to look at some rooms here."

"I am sure you will take great pleasure in seeing them." Señor Gutierres had bounded to the door in his eagerness, but Señor Ramirez held his hand up in the air.

"Before the rooms," he said, "we are all going to have a drink together to celebrate the arrival of a lady. Champagne for her, Gutierres. Sit down, Señorita."

Señorita Córdoba complied with this request only too willingly and took her seat at the bar.

"How delightful," she said. "I always like to drink champagne because it reminds me of Paris, where I belong."

"Paris is a very gay city. The night life there is very beautiful," said Señor Gutierres, believing that he was dealing with an elegant client. "Here in this hotel there is everything to remind you of Paris. I have letters from there asking for reservations. Your father no doubt owns a finca, and you no doubt have lived all your life in Paris and in Biarritz. And now you find this country strange, like the jungle – *bien?*"

"This lady," said Señor Ramirez, "lives in the pension where I always put my wife and my two girls. That is how I know her."

Gutierres' face fell. He had hardly expected to draw his customers from Señora Espinoza's pension, which he considered a step below the large touristic hotels.

"I know the lady who owns the pension," he said sadly, "but very little, only to speak to. I know very few people in this town. My servants buy for me, so why should I speak to anyone?"

"You are better off keeping your life to yourself," said Señorita Córdoba, "than having companions that are doing nothing but just sitting and trying to find someone to laugh with."

A shadow seemed to pass across the face of Señor Ramirez. For a moment he thought of going back to the capital right away. "Here, here," he shouted. "What is all this about your life alone? Let's be together, friends – like baby chickens under the wings of the mother hen."

Señor Gutierres was now just a little bit drunk, and he was beginning to wander on to things that he scarcely knew he thought about. "No," he said, "no – no chickens under one wing. Each man alone, proud, acting as he has been taught to act by his family, never living in a house that is lower than the house in which he was born. Each man remembering his father and his mother and what he has been taught is sacred."

"The only thing that is sacred, my poor boy, is money," said the pleasure-seeking Norberto.

"No, it is one's class," insisted Señor Gutierres. "We must love our own class. I cannot talk and be friendly with people whose childhood I know has been different from mine, who did not have the same silver on the table when they sat down to eat."

"You would be glad to talk with me, Gutierres, even if I ate with pigs when I was a little boy."

"No, no, I would not. There is real friendship only between men who have always been used to the same things. Between two such men no words need be spoken, because each one knows that the other will do nothing to disgust him or upset him, and the pleasure of being with such a friend is quite enough. I have such a friend here, who knows the value of every piece of furniture in the Alhambra. And there is no wine that is familiar to me that is not familiar to him. We don't have to say anything to each other. Each of us remembers the same things. His family and my family come from the same part of Spain. I feel so close to him that I might say that I would even wear his underclothes. Forgive me, Señorita." He bowed his head.

"But *my* underwear you would not put on for five thousand quetzales, eh, señor?" said Ramirez, throwing his chest out.

Señor Gutierres, having started off talking about his thin code which he considered to be a universal and important ideology, had necessarily to go on further. His astute business sense was completely obliterated by the fanaticism that all men feel about whatever it is they believe makes the world an orderly and respectable place in which to live. "No, señor," he said, "I would not wear your underwear, for your education is far below mine and your family, as I know, were not much more than peasants before they came to this country."

"Oh, how rude you are," said Señorita Córdoba, taking hold of Señor Ramirez' hand. "And I am sure it is not true."

"Certainly it is true," said Señor Ramirez, "and this monkey will soon find out what else is true." Señorita Córdoba was surprised that Señor Ramirez had as yet not kicked the bar stools over, but apparently his family was not a sensitive point with him, and perhaps also he was having a very pleasurable reaction from the drinks and was not inclined to fight.

"Let him kiss his chairs," continued Señor Ramirez, "and see how many women he will get to kiss. He is probably a miserable eunuch anyway. Kiss me." He put his hand under Señorita Córdoba's chin and kissed her full on the mouth. Señorita Córdoba wondered whether or not she should resist this kiss, and decided very quickly it was wiser to pretend to enjoy it. She passed a fluttering hand over his ear, which was one of the few love gestures she knew about.

"This woman is a trollop," said Señor Gutierres in a trembling voice. Señor Ramirez could not possibly let this remark pass so he stopped kissing Señorita Córdoba and gave Gutierres a sock on the jaw that knocked him off his stool and onto the floor where he lay unconscious.

"Now," he said to Señorita Córdoba, lifting her down from her stool, "let us find an agreeable place in this beautiful Alhambra Hotel." He spat on the floor.

"Oh, well," said Señorita Córdoba, deciding that it was time for her to be a little bit shy. "Shall we stand in the patio a little bit and then go home?"

"No," he said. "I want to go where I can see your beautiful face." He led her upstairs, and with his foot he kicked open the door to one of the bedrooms, and turned on the light. She went and sat down on one of the chairs which Señor Gutierres considered to be beautiful and folded her hands in her lap. "I have always been interested to know a man like you," she said, "with such a wonderful way of knowing how to live."

"There are no disappointments in my life," said Señor Ramirez, "and I love it. I can show you some wonderful things."

"My life is a terrible disappointment to me," said Señorita Córdoba, and her heart beat very quickly as she felt she was approaching her goal.

The room was badly lighted and she searched his eyes avidly to see what effect her words had made on him. It seemed to her that they had a slightly blank look, like the eyes of someone who is gazing at a particular object without really seeing it.

"You have not had the right kind of love," he said.

"That is not the only reason," said Señorita Córdoba, shaking her head vigorously. Señor Ramirez was feeling suddenly very drunk and he threw himself down on the bed.

"You must not go to sleep," she said nervously, rising to her feet.

"Who in the devil is going to sleep?" Señor Ramirez leaned on his elbows and looked at her like an angry bull.

"Listen," she said, "I'm so miserable on that finca where I am living that I think that if it goes on any longer I will certainly drown myself in the river."

"Drowning is no good," said Ramirez. "That's only good for scared fools, like those little dogs that shiver all the time – they have them in Mexico. You are not on your finca now. Come here on the bed and stop talking so much." He put his arm out and caught at the air with his hand.

"I want to go away to Paris, where I have friends, and start a dress shop."

"Sure," said Señor Ramirez.

"But I have not got any money."

"I have so much money."

"I need five thousand dollars."

He started to unbutton his pants. Señorita Córdoba remembered that many men were not interested in ladies nearly as much after they had made love to them as they were beforehand, so she decided that she had better make sure that she received a check first. She did not know how to do this tactfully but her own greed and the fact that he was drunk, and that she thought him a coarse person anyway, made her believe that she would be successful. She walked quickly to the window and stood with her back to him.

"What are you looking at outside the window?" asked Señor Ramirez, in a thick voice, smelling trouble.

"I am not looking at anything. On the contrary, I am just thinking about you, and how little you are really interested in whether or not I will open a dress shop."

"You can open a thousand dress shops, my beautiful woman. What is the matter with you?"

"You lie. I cannot even open one dress shop." She turned around and faced him.

"Wildcat," he said to her.

She tried to look more touching. "You will not help me to open a dress shop. Must it be someone else that will help me?"

"I am going to help you open fifty dress shops – tomorrow."

"I would not ask you for fifty, only for one. Would you make me happy and give me a check tonight so that I know when I go to sleep I will have my dress shop? I would like to sleep in peace just for once and know that I am not going to have to go back to that terrible finca, and listen to the dogs howling and my mother praying out loud. This one check would banish all these horrible things from my mind right away and I would be eternally grateful to you. I would be so glad that it had been you who did it, too."

"Well, then, come here."

She sat down on the bed beside him and he kissed her, but while he was kissing her she pushed him away and said to him, "Give me the check now."

"What is this?" asked Señor Ramirez. "Are you still talking about this damn foolish check?"

"Yes," said Señorita Córdoba, seeing that it was no use any longer to employ tact. "I will not go to bed with you unless you first give me a check for five thousand quetzales, or a piece of paper saying that you owe this sum of money to me."

Certainly this remark was not having the right effect on Señor Ramirez, who struggled with difficulty down from the bed and buttoned his trousers. She watched him attentively and noticed that the glands in his neck were moving. "Angry again," she said to herself, but she could think of nothing to say that would calm him except "Where are you going?" which she asked in a rather ironical tone of voice, all her false ardor dampened now by her own conviction that she would fail to get her money. Señor Ramirez was trembling and very red in the face. She stood still and appeared to be very calm even when he finally stumbled out of the room, but when she heard him clambering down the stairs she walked out onto the balcony and looked down over the railing into the patio. One light was burning and in a moment Señor Ramirez came into the patio and picked up what she saw was a large urn with a tall plant growing out of it. This he threw to the ground not very far from his feet, because it was very heavy. It smashed in many pieces, but made less noise than she expected to hear because the dirt inside the urn muffled the sound that it would otherwise have made.

She could not understand his fury, knowing so little about deeply outraged feelings and the fact that so much of people's violence is spent in the elaborate and grim protection of a personality as undeveloped as a fœtus yet grown quickly to tremendous proportions, like a giant weed. Being stupid herself, she did not recognize the danger inherent in all those whose self-protective instincts are far greater than the personality they are protecting, because their armor can only be timeworn and made up of the most stagnating of human impulses. Señorita Córdoba was unwounded if unintelligent, and her rages were unimportant nervous discharges.

Señor Ramirez was struggling with the big wooden doors that led into the street and making a terrible racket shaking the heavy iron chains, but it was to no avail because the doors were locked from the inside. She could only hear him now without being able to see him, since the bulb threw no light into the front of the patio. Suddenly he stopped rattling the chains and she heard him walking back in the direction of the staircase.

"My God," she thought, "he has murder in his heart, certainly," and she sneaked around to another side of the balcony. Fortunately the servant who had before been looking for the chicken was awakened by the noise and she now came into the patio to find out what the trouble was. "The door is locked," Ramirez shouted at her.

"Yes," she whispered. "I'll fetch the key."

She returned with the key and let Señor Ramirez out of the patio into the street. Señorita Córdoba decided to wait a little while before returning to the pension herself. She was thinking very hard of a way to redeem herself on the following day. She was like certain mediocre politically minded persons upon whose minds failure leaves no deep impression, not because of any burning belief in the ideal for which they are fighting, but rather because they are accustomed to thinking only of what to do next. These people are often valuable but at the same time so removed from reality that they are ridiculous. After sitting a while in the gloomy Spanish bedroom Señorita Córdoba went downstairs and in turn awakened the Indian servant, who let her out.

LAURIE COLWIN

Old Flames

AT THE AUTUMN cocktail party of the *Journal of American Finance*, Freddie Delielle ran smack into James Clemens, whom she had not seen for two years. He was wearing one of his beautiful tweed jackets, and the ridiculously long paisley scarf he had always affected was wound around his neck. At his left was a hefty-looking black man wearing a white skullcap, striped trousers, and a long tan linen shift.

On James' right was a girl so blond and pretty she caused Freddie, who was dark and plain, to blink. The girl wore a fuzzy red sweater, dangling earrings, and lipstick to match her nail polish. She and James looked so splendid together that it was hard for Freddie to believe that at one time James had been her own illicit lover.

Freddie was wearing her nine-month-old son, William, whom she carried in a hip sling. He was a very cheerful baby, who clutched a rubber giraffe in one hand and a teething biscuit in the other. Crumbs from his biscuit ornamented his mother's skirt.

James came right over and gave them a hard stare. He looked almost angry. Before Freddie could stop herself, she asked James, "Who's the dish?"

James' features instantly relaxed. A smile lit his face.

"That's Dr. Milton Obutu," he said. "I know you've been reading his articles on the economic history of the developing nations with avid interest.

"The other one."

"Oh," James said. "A recent acquisition. Speaking of which, you seem to have acquired a little something yourself."

"This is my son, William," Freddie said. "He's nine months old."

James leaned over and peered at William, who hid his face in his mother's neck.

"Not very friendly," James said.

"Don't be shy, Will," Freddie said. "Show your face, please."

William looked up and began to spit.

"He has your social style, I see," said James. "What a very good-looking boy."

"He looks like his father."

"He looks like you," James said. "Of course, I am less intimately connected with the way his father looks."

Freddie felt her cheeks flush.

"So," she said. "I see you've found my replacement. A much better model and much nicer color."

The beautiful blond girl was deep in conversation with Dr. Obutu. Her hair was swept up in a French twist and she wore an enormous gold bracelet.

"How interesting that after throwing me over you're actually jealous," said James.

Freddie found that she could not look him in the eye.

"Dr. Obutu seems very familiar," she said. "Did he win a prize or something?"

"I see motherhood has not made you any keener on current events," said James. "He won the Valeur Medal in economics. But not to change the subject, I never knew that jealousy was included in your emotional repertoire. Of course, I had no idea you were fixing to have a baby. How little we know!"

ONCE UPON A TIME Freddie and James had known an enormous number of things about each other. Freddie, who liked to keep her head uncluttered, had ended up knowing the names of all James' friends, their wives and children, as well as everyone connected with his wife, Vera. She knew the details of Vera's accomplishments as an interior designer, and the names of all the people whose houses, offices, beach cabañas, villas, lofts, and compounds she had worked on. She knew where Vera bought her clothes and where James had his shirts made, and all about his former colleagues in the investment-banking house from which James had prematurely retired. She heard endless stories about his landlady in the South of France, where he and Vera had rented a summer house for the past fifteen years.

It was harder for James to get information out of Freddie, but he had his methods. He was not above snooping into her mail or opening her cupboards and drawers. Unfortunately, these did not reveal much, except that she and Grey, her husband, drank tea and ate Irish oatmeal, had several pairs of hiking boots, two fishing rods, and a butterfly net, and that they got mail from a number of nature societies.

It had taken James a long time to learn that Freddie had known Grey almost all her life; they had met at school in London, where both their fathers had been sent by their firms. You would think, James often said, that a person might reveal one or two of these not very personal details, but Freddie was a clam. She felt it was a betrayal to tell James anything, whereas James took the opposite tack. Information *defused* things, he felt. If he nattered on endlessly about his family, he could con himself into thinking that there was nothing odd about the way he was feeling. As a consequence, he sang like a canary.

They never discussed the reason for their love affair or its effect on their lives. They had broken up numerous times, but their last parting two years ago had been final. Freddie, as was customary, did the initiating. She said, with a tone of resolve in her voice James had never heard before, "My life is being ruined."

Naturally, she did not say how it was being ruined, but James knew the knell of finality when he heard it. He had been listening for it all along, and when it came he was not entirely unrelieved.

While his life was not being ruined, it was made complicated in a way he often found unbearable. Now he was used to missing Freddie. It was rather like a chronic pain of the lower back. But when he looked at her and her child a feeling akin to rage overtook him.

"I always said you'd leave me in the dust," he said.

Freddie was silent.

"You threw me over," James said.

"I did not," Freddie said. James was pleased to see that there were tears in her eyes. "We were bound to part, one way or the other."

"We were?" James said. "Not from where I sat."

"Come off it, Jim," said Freddie, who alone in the world addressed James thus. "The only thing our relationship disturbed was us. I left you sitting in your ornamental house surrounded by your loving family and thousands of friends and relations."

At the sound of the sharp tone in his mother's voice, William began to fidget. "He's getting bored," Freddie said. "I'm going to have to take him away soon."

"Fine," said James. "I'll take you both away for a drink, and we can continue this conversation."

"What about your friend?"

"Ishbelle?" James said. "She's very enterprising. She's writing a profile of Dr. Obutu for the *Wall Street Journal*."

"Ishbelle?" said Freddie.

"She's half English, half Dutch."

"And won't she think it's odd that you're leaving with me?"

"I'll take care of it," James said. "Besides, you're a woman with a baby. What could be more safe and respectable?"

FREDDIE AND JAMES in their winter coats ambled to the corner. James took her by the arm. The air was chilly and wet, and it was getting dark. William relaxed against his mother, and Freddie knew he was falling asleep.

"Here we are," James said, leading her through a wooden door.

Freddie had had hundreds of meals with James, mostly in out-of-the-way delicatessens, Chinese restaurants, or coffee shops. In the beginning James had attempted to take Freddie to decent restaurants and was so often rebuffed that he had given up.

Now she found herself in a bar full of polished blond wood, with a fire burning in the grate and fresh flowers in an ornamental urn.

"Do you come here often?" Freddie said.

"Once in a while."

"We never went to places like this."

"Not for lack of trying," James said.

They took a table with a banquette. William's eyes were closed, so Freddie spread a little blanket, unzipped his snowsuit, and set him down to take a nap. She took off his hat and kissed his hair.

"Ah, motherhood," James said. "In the old days you used to throw your keys into the pocket of one of your hideous jackets and off we'd go. Now I see you carry a little mother bag with a blanket inside, and probably diapers, toys, and bottles, too. How well organized you've become! Why, just days ago, it seems, you allowed me to wonder what sort of child *we'd* produce."

Freddie had very accurate recall and reminded James that this had been his exclusive fantasy.

"You played your own small part," James said.

"Stop trying to make me feel more awful than I feel, Jim."

"I don't believe you feel awful," James said. "You let me go without so much as a God-damned by-your-leave."

"We had a million by-your-leaves," Freddie said. "Besides, you had your baby. In fact, you had two."

James looked at her with an expression Freddie had often suffered as fatherly tenderness. It made her wince.

"All right," James said. "As long as you ditched me for family life, you may as well tell me about it. How did it go?"

Freddie had heard James' birth stories countless times. His son Quentin had been born in Paris on New Year's Eve and the doctor had set off a bottle of champagne in the delivery room. Aaron was a labor so fast he had almost been born in a taxicab.

Freddie, on the other hand, had been hospitalized for toxemia two weeks before William's birth, and William had been born by Cæsarean section. He had been slightly underweight and made to stay in the hospital for eight days after Freddie was released. It had felt like eight months. Freddie knew she had not quite gotten over it and she was reluctant to tell James anything at all, but once she started she found she could not stop. James leaned back in his chair and listened with no particular expression on his face.

"And the baby's father?" he said conversationally.

"Are you referring to my husband, Grey?" Freddie said.

"You speak as if you had done this all yourself," James said.

Freddie stared at him. Did he really want to hear her tell him how wonderful Grey had been, how he had taken a month's leave of absence from work and had barely left her and William except to run errands? How patient he was, how tender and besotted, and how jubilant he was to have the baby home? "He's an excellent father," she said.

"And are you finding motherhood very fulfilling?" James said.

"It's very public."

"As opposed to your previous activities."

"For instance," Freddie said, "if I take William to the bank and he begins to squawl, at least three people give me advice – to feed him, or give him a toy, or to prop him up in his stroller. When I took *you* to the bank, no one told me anything like that."

James sipped his drink in silence. "How things change," he said. "No more charming dalliance in that study of yours, which I assume is now the child's room."

"It isn't. We had that spare room, which is warmer."

"A snug family group," said James.

"You're snug enough, Jim," Freddie said. "Didn't you use to drag me by the hair over to your little snuggery and show me album after album of happy-family portraits? Don't be so mingy."

"I'm not," James said. "Your baby is awake."

William peered up from the banquette. His cheek was pink from sleeping on it. Freddie took him into her arms. "You're a hungry boy," she said.

James suddenly looked alarmed. "I don't suppose you were or are one of those nurse-your-baby-in-public types," he said.

"Yup," Freddie said. "But don't you worry. I've got a nice bottle in my bag."

The lights of the bar gave the room an orange glow. Freddie bent over her baby, who drank his bottle peacefully and stared up at her. Her hair fell into her eyes, but she did not have a free hand to push it away. James restrained himself from doing it for her.

"A tender scene," he said. "I wonder what sort of parent you are. Probably no-nonsense. Schedules, enforced naps, and so on."

Freddie, who found the experience of having a baby exactly like being madly in love, looked up at James.

"I only treated *you* that way," she said. "Actually, I'm a very indulgent mother."

"It's funny what we didn't know about one another," James said.

"It's entirely appropriate to the situation," said Freddie.

William had finished his bottle and was sitting on his mother's lap trying to take all the silverware off the table. Freddie reached into her bag and pulled out his rubber giraffe and a set of plastic keys. When they both looked up, James could see what a replica of his mother William was. Freddie kissed her baby's neck and he began to laugh. A look James had never seen before appeared on Freddie's face. James sighed. He felt weak and depleted, as if after a long swim.

"It's time to go," Freddie said.

"One more thing," said James. "I've always wanted to know. When you and I snuck off to Vermont for our little trip when Vera and Grey were away, what did you tell Grey?"

She looked suddenly so stricken that James realized their trip had been the occasion of the first lie Freddie had ever told her husband.

"Never mind," he said.

Freddie pushed the air off her forehead. She felt rather exhausted herself. "O.K., William," she said. "It's time for the horrible torture of your snowsuit."

She set William down on the banquette and started with his feet. He began to squirm. Then he began to cry.

"They all hate this," Freddie said to James.

"Ours didn't."

"Really?" Freddie said. "How totally unusual."

Finally William was bundled up and fastened into his hip carrier. James threw some money on the table, and they ambled into the street.

It was misty and dark; halos formed around the street lamps.

"It feels like snow," said James. "It's very odd seeing you."

Freddie was silent.

"Is it odd seeing me?" he said.

"Yes," said Freddie.

"I had forgotten what a rewarding conversationalist you are," James said. "I suppose that with all your motherly chores you no longer wonder what we were doing together."

"I think about it a lot," Freddie said.

"And what brilliant thoughts have you had?"

"Love seeketh only self to please," Freddie said.

"What's that supposed to mean?"

"It's a quote from William Blake. Now I get to ask you a question."

"Anything," James said. Freddie had never been one for a direct question.

"Where did you get the paisley scarf?"

"Is that all you wanted to know?"

"Sort of."

"It belonged to Vera's grandfather, who was quite a dandy," James said. "I'd be happy to give it to you as a goodbye present. You can keep it for William and I can say I lost it."

"Oh, no!" said Freddie. "I always think of you in that scarf."

FINALLY THE THREE of them reached the corner. James was

about to hail a taxi when Freddie grabbed his arm. "Are you in love with that girl?" she said.

James spun around. "What's it to you?"

"I want to know," Freddie said. Her voice was shaking.

James looked down at her intently.

"Are you?" Freddie said. She was clutching his arm rather painfully.

"She's my daughter-in-law," James said. "Aaron got married last year."

Freddie let go. James saw that her face was flooded with relief, which was instantly supplanted by anger. "You bastard," she said.

"It shouldn't make any difference to you one way or the other," James said. "Now that you're a respectable wife and mother."

"Are you in love with anyone else?" Freddie said.

James did not have to repress the desire to kiss her: it was not easy to contemplate kissing a woman who was holding a baby. Instead, he hung his scarf around her neck and pulled her a little closer. William found this very entertaining and began to laugh. "Does that mean that if I can't be in love with you I also can't be in love with anyone else?" he said.

"I didn't mean that," said Freddie, slipping out from under the scarf.

"I think you did," James said. A few fine snowflakes began to fall. "I'll get you a taxi, so your precious darling doesn't get wet."

James hailed a taxi and opened the door. He bent to kiss Freddie goodbye. She thought she heard him say, "You were the only one."

She ducked her head, so instead of kissing Freddie, James kissed William, and as he watched them drive away he could still smell that clear, benign baby smell of biscuits and talcum powder.

ANN BEATTIE

Cards

SOMETIME DURING THE MOVE from Chicago to New York, just before Josie moved in with Philip Neuveville, she took back her maiden name. I hadn't seen her for a couple of years; when we met again she told me, murmuring as shyly as a young girl asked to dance, that she wasn't Josie Runoff anymore, but Josephine Willoughby.

I've known Josie for nine years, off and on, and it's nice to be in the same city with her again. We often meet for lunch. Today, her pale hair, subtly streaked, touches her shoulders and waves away from her face, making her amber eyes seem larger. No blush on her high cheekbones, pearl earrings, only gloss on her lips. A little tortoiseshell half-moon holds back her bangs. The waiter is impressed. So is the water boy. So are the men at the table to our left. Josie is writing down her recipe for seviche, on the Z page of her book of phone numbers. She gives the impression that nothing much bothers her – including ripping a page out of her pretty, fabric-covered phone book. She does not look up when the waiter puts down our glasses of Pinot Noir.

"Those men think we're pathetic," I whisper.

"I don't think that's what they're thinking."

"Oh, you think all these boring men have minds swirling like Casanova's. You know what they're thinking about? Getting their son into Dartmouth. Then they're wondering whether they should order a new office chair in black or gray."

"No, they aren't. They're wondering what perfume you have on, and whether you now hate your husband so much because he voted for Reagan that you'd do anything behind his back in the afternoon."

"They're thinking about the big beds at the Helmsley."

"Or the UN Plaza," she says. "And they're feeling very sophisticated because everyone hasn't discovered it. Afterward, they want to go downstairs and swim, right?"

The waiter brings the first course. Josie is having pâté. I'm having borscht, which I'm sure I'll get on my silk blouse. I can already feel the specks of soup flying out of the bowl, like sand in the wind. I stir the sour cream, reluctant to begin.

Josie leans across the table and whispers, "They had money on whether we'd order white wine and arugula salad."

We always eat big lunches. We hate the idea that people might think of us as two ladies who sit around eating broiled sole and frosted grapes. Last week we went to a Greek restaurant for moussaka and lots of bread and butter.

The water boy pours water into my glass.

"I was wrong," she says, buttering a roll. "We do have *Grand Hotel* on tape. Come over Friday and see it. Bring Max."

"He's in Germany."

"Oh, God, why does he travel so much? Philip loves to sit around with Max, and he's never in town. Philip's embarrassed to admit that he misses people; I said that to him, and he drew himself up and said that the only reason he was so interested in Max's whereabouts was because it was clear Max was in the CIA. I thought that CIA hysteria died down years ago. It did with everybody else." She finishes her wine. "What's he doing in Germany?" she says.

One of the four men – the best looking – has turned sideways to listen.

"He's looking over the audit of some company his company does business with."

"You come anyway," she says. "Philip ordered a case of this stuff." She points to her empty glass. The waiter comes to her side and puts down her plate of lamb chops. He moves to my side of the table and puts down my lobster salad. Another waiter asks if we want more wine.

"No, thank you," she says.

The man at the other table crosses his legs. He takes a cigarette out of a silver case and puts it in his mouth. Another man reaches across the table to light it.

"What did Max do about that young woman who was in love with him?"

"I don't know."

"She was calling all the time when you were over there."

"And when I wasn't, I'm sure."

"What did he do?" Josie says, pushing the watercress away from her second lamb chop with her finger.

"I don't know. I'm not sure the calls have stopped. She started calling him after almost a year."

"I hope I never do that," Josie says.

"That's the perfect opening for me to pretend to be dumb."

"Why? You think it's impossible that I'd do something like that?"

"No. I was just going to say, 'Why would you call Max?'"

"I'll tell you," she says, wiping her mouth, "if you weren't involved with him, I would."

The dishes are cleared away. I order coffee. "Two," Josie says.

Almost instantly, the water boy comes toward the table, cups and saucers held high, steam rising. He puts the coffees on the table, then backs up, waits a second, and goes to get cream and sugar. The man sitting sideways raises his finger for the bill. The steam rising from my coffee comes as high as my chin before it thins and wisps away.

"Philip's CIA craziness," Josie says. "And bringing up marriage just to say that he doesn't see the point of marriage. I could do without either of those routines." She takes another sip of coffee, looks up, and smiles. "Remember the four of us snowed in at your aunt's house in Saratoga? We never thought we'd get out. We had those borrowed skis, and you and I went out until we were bow-legged with pain. I remember that huge picture window she had, with the leather seat cushions. Sitting there with our legs stretched out, looking at the birds flying to the suet ball."

"The kamikaze squirrel."

"Ned liking his tent so much that he went out and pitched it in that blizzard," she says.

Ned and I have been divorced for three years, and I still turn to stone when his name is spoken. I can see how I must appear to others: exaggerated calm, fingers delicately hovering above the rim of the coffee cup, as if I were playing chess. Ned pitching the tent. Ned stalking the squirrel, pointing a broken branch with an alligator-head kitchen mitt on the end. The snow that fell for two days, constantly. Josie was married to Jack Runoff. He loved Beethoven and pretended to love Mozart. The next year they were divorced and he was under indictment for fraud, but the case was dismissed. Ned and Jack had been together in Korea. They considered each other brothers, but Ned couldn't stand classical music. He listened almost exclusively to the Rolling Stones. Once, by pure coincidence, Josie bought Jack a red turtleneck and I bought Ned the same sweater. They got together, and each had on the same thing. Neither ever wore his sweater again.

"I wonder if Ned's still into his wilderness adventures," I say.

"Yeah, he still is," she says, sipping her coffee.

"What do you mean?"

"He still wants to spend every free moment camping. Still talks about the sky as if he just discovered it yesterday."

"How do you know that?" I say.

"Oh, because – oh, why pretend to pass over it? It's the strangest thing. I didn't look him up, God knows. I went to the optometrist with Philip. He can't see a thing after drops are put in his eyes, and he's like a child. I was in the waiting room, and Ned walked in. He'd scratched his cornea, riding his bike in Central Park. He'd just moved to town, and he'd caught a branch in the face. He was surprised to see me, too. It was awkward. He wasn't sure. He was looking at me with one eye."

"What did he say?"

"Well, you know, it was awkward. He asked how I was, and I asked how he was. Then Philip came out, and right away he started to feel like he was going to faint. He put his hand out and Ned helped him into a chair. The nurse went in and got the doctor. Philip was so embarrassed. He's such a child."

"Was he all right?"

"It was only eye drops. They wear off in an hour."

"Ned."

"Oh. Yes. It turned out to be nothing serious. One of Philip's clients had insisted that his driver bring us over to the doctor's, so we dropped Ned at his office too. On the ride, he and Philip discovered that they both passed up working on the same account. They got together after that and had lunch. Philip had him over to dinner. I thought we'd see him once, and that would be that."

"Did he bring somebody to dinner?"

"Well, of course he did. You've been divorced for years, haven't you?" She sighs. "We just see them every couple of weeks."

"You see him every two weeks? How long – "

"I didn't want to talk about it and depress you," she says. "I felt awkward, though. As though I were doing something sneaky." She brushes her hair off her shoulder. "He's Philip's friend, not mine."

"If you want me to be magnanimous and say that there's no reason why he shouldn't be your friend, I can't do that. I don't think he should be your friend."

"He isn't. They go up to Philip's brother's place in Maine. I don't go."

"What do you do?" I say.

"Well, what do you think I do? Sleep with him?"

"I didn't say that. And it's rather insulting – "

"Oh, don't say 'rather,'" she says, reaching across the table and clasping my wrist. "I can't tell Philip whom to have for a friend and whom not to have."

"You do remember how crazy he was," I say.

"He wasn't crazy, he was mean."

"He's not anymore?"

"He's pleasant. I'm pleasant. What do you think I should do?"

"I'm sorry," I say.

"You don't have any reason to apologize. It's awkward. To tell the truth, the real problem is that I won't stand up to Philip. I just said that Ned was somebody I'd known slightly years ago, because I could tell right away that he liked him. He always says I don't like anybody he likes. So I'm trying to be nice. I'm trying to convince him that he should marry me."

"He should."

"He should, but no matter what a good little girl I am, he won't. He would have married me before this, if he'd decided to do it."

"He loves you, though," I say.

"Yes," she says. "And Max loves you."

Our hands are folded on the table. The waiter moves slowly into Josie's peripheral vision. She turns toward him, reaching for the bill.

"It's mine," I say.

"I know it's tacky to fight over checks," she says, taking the check from the waiter, "but I feel so awful. Let me treat you to lunch."

"What do you have to feel awful about?"

"Having said anything at all. But you know – if you found out, you'd think I was a traitor or something. It was just one of those bizarre things."

She unzips her handbag one-handed, clamping it against her with her elbow. "If it will make you feel better, thank you," I say.

"Good," she says.

The waiter takes the tray. His pants legs are slightly different lengths; they're rolled at the cuff, not sewn. He is wearing orthopedic shoes. He takes the check from our table and from the men's table. He hurries across the room and comes back, bowing as he puts the little tray back on the table. He goes to the other table. The water boy is there, pouring water.

I'm reaching for my shoulder bag when the man at the next table says, "Josephine Runoff." Josie and I both snap our heads around. The man is smiling. "I don't know what your credit line is, so I'm afraid I'll have to return this," he says.

By mistake, the waiter has put Josie's card on the man's tray. He holds it out, but sees that she can't reach it. Both start to rise. His white napkin falls on the floor. He walks to our table, smiling.

"Thank you," she says.

He lifts his card off our tray. "The bills are right," he says. "Just mixed up the cards."

"You may be sorry," she says. "My line of credit is excellent."

"And so is the food here," he says. "Have you eaten here before?"

"Often," Josie says.

"Good restaurant," he says again. "We've started coming here just about every other day."

We both smile. Subtle, but the message has registered: this is the place to find him.

The waiter, seeing us talking, suspects his error and hurries to the table.

"It's fine," the man says. "A problem easily solved. I was sure I wasn't Josephine Runoff."

We get our coats. I leave a dollar in the big brass bowl. The maître d' opens the door. Outside, the street is dotted with bright-yellow taxis. People moving in all directions. A nurse passes by, pushing a stroller. A messenger zigs and zags through honking traffic, pedaling the bicycle with no hands.

"Get the feeling that that man's not going to forget your name?" I say. Josie and I are walking close together, in the wind.

"It won't do him any good," she says. "I'm not Josephine Runoff. I'm Josephine Willoughby, who wants to be Ms. Willoughby-Neuveville." She shakes her head. "Isn't it all silly?" she says. "Being this age and wanting so much to change? Waiting isn't one of my virtues. Not so long ago, I would have flirted. Let a few days pass, then gone back there for lunch. We would have gone to – where did you say? The Helmsley."

"Would you really have done that?"

"Probably," she says. She smiles. She reaches in her pocket, takes something out, and holds it in front of us.

"Back at the office, full of hope," she sighs.

"His business card?" I say, reaching for it. "The man in the restaurant?"

"Of course you realize that he asked the waiter to make the mistake," she says.

"When did he give you this?" I say. "Why didn't you tell me?"

"I am telling you. He palmed it to me underneath my American Express card." She takes it back, drops it in her pocket again, and links arms with me. "That excites men, doesn't it?" she says. "Pulling off something sneaky and acting blasé." She's looking at the sidewalk, and I see her smile before the wind whips her hair across her face. "They just don't know," she says. "We do it all the time."

ELIZABETH TALLENT

Black Holes

JUNIPER AND JADE CLARK, who are twins, hog the windows in the station wagon's back seat, so that Fanny Giles, unwilling to climb over Jade's legs to get to the middle, is stranded for a moment on the school sidewalk. "Get in, Fanny," Mrs. Clark urges from behind the steering wheel. "Don't be shy." She leans forward and squints until she can see Fanny, whose red hair, backlit, has been drawn into a severe French braid that makes her small, sharp face even smaller and sharper; the wan, nutmeg freckles are so numerous that there are stray flecks between the spikes of her lower lashes. Her upper lip has the dusty cast peculiar to fair redheads, but her eyes are dark and the wings of her nostrils are pinkened as if by a cold. Looking at Fanny, Mrs. Clark thinks two things: Fanny is scared, and Fanny's mother must have been a fox.

"That's not shy," Jade says. "That's stupid. Climb in, Fanny-Panny. Nobody's going to tell on you. That's the law of the car pool."

"Tell what?" Mrs. Clark says as Fanny works her way into the seat. "No, don't say a word. I don't want to know."

"Oh, God!" Jade says. Fanny has nicked Jade's leg with the corner of her lunchbox, and a small hole blooms in the knee of Jade's black tights.

"No profanity in this car, not while I'm driving," Mrs. Clark says. "I don't care what your father lets you get away with."

Juniper breathes a cloud across her window and writes "ADAM." Jade, after glancing over her shoulder, fogs her window and writes "ADAM LOVES JADE." Juniper makes tongue prints; Jade draws a dozen deft "X"s, for kisses. Caught between them, awed by the twins' cold second-grade glamour, Fanny feels herself whittled down to a ragged scarecrow, with the note that her kindergarten teacher asked her to take home weighing like lead in her pocket. When Mrs. Clark brakes the station wagon abruptly and faces Fanny, Fanny wishes she could either disappear or turn into one of the twins, who are paying no attention to their mother.

"Hey, Fanny," Mrs. Clark says. "That's your new house, isn't it?" She points. Fanny looks up a sweep of gopher-pocked lawn to the house, its long porch trimmed with weathered gingerbread; there is a pane missing in the window to the left of the front door. She nods yes.

"So?" Mrs. Clark says.

"So?" Jade echoes, absently mocking her mother, then writing on her window, "BORING!!"

"So do you think you'll like living there, Fanny?" Mrs. Clark persists.

Juniper erases her window with the heel of her hand. "What if she doesn't – what's she going to do about it?"

"I like it," Fanny says softly.

"We're going to miss you," Mrs. Clark tells her. "We'll miss coming home from school with you."

"I won't," Jade says.

Biting her lower lip to concentrate, Juniper writes in the fog on her window, "HELP!"

SATURDAY MORNING, Will Giles blows the blue-black husks of dead flies from the channel in the window sash before gently pressing the new pane of glass into place. His reflection slants across it – a dark-haired man on his knees, looking hopeful. The glass fits, and the panes of the tall sidelight to the left of the front door are complete. He smiles over his shoulder at Fanny, who is sitting on the porch railing swinging her heels, and then he knocks on the door. "In a week, you'll be inside, and maybe you'll hear somebody knock, and you'll feel nice and safe because you know whoever's there is knocking on solid oak. Isn't it a great front door, Fanny?"

Fanny is five, child of a marriage Will thinks of, with a blitheness he would immediately distrust in one of his analysands, as well forgotten. In fact, he has a recurring dream that he is in a booth trying to find enough change to call Oklahoma City, where Ally has lived since the divorce. She didn't think it very likely that she would keep in touch with him or Fanny. Ally had wanted to make a clean sweep of her previous existence and she seems to have stuck by that resolve. Will hasn't heard from her in a year.

Fanny is rocking on the railing, left leg cradled to her chest, the knee tucked under her chin. He reaches for a screwdriver, and taps her foot with it. "Hey, you look a little precarious."

"I can sit like this hours and not fall."

"Don't be so hard on my heart, Fanny."

She straightens, going as primly alert as if an invisible book had descended to her head, and squeezes first one dirty sneaker, then the other, into the narrow gaps between the spindles that support the railing, daring him to tell her not to do that, either; when he doesn't, she looks satisfied, and locks her feet, toed in, behind a peeling spindle.

"Thank you," he says. "Once this is finished, your house is going to be in good shape." Since she's been coming here with him on Saturdays, he has taken to calling it her house. A truer joke might be that for a long time to come this is going to be the bank's house. His second wife, Carrie Ann, argued that they couldn't keep Christopher's crib at the end of the hallway for long, that a baby and a five-year-old really need a room each. This costly Victorian, with its leaks and loose shingles, with swallows' nests suspended in its sooty chimneys, was her solution. Will is not in love with it, not the way his wife is, but he has begun to feel for it that involuntary affection sparked in him by things badly in need of repair.

"I thought there was still lots of stuff to do," Fanny says.

He begins to limn the new pane with the tube of glazing compound. "No," he says, "this is all I wanted to get to" – and feels pleased and provident, having timed the last urgent repair for the last Saturday before they move in.

She jumps from the railing and slides by him, leaving the door open. With a razor blade he trims a gauzy line of glazing compound into a neat margin, pausing now and then to admire the door, which, because a shaft of sun has crossed the porch, blazes: old oak with its curls and knots and close grain, the gold hidden within the sombre wood like flakes of precious metal in a stream, cartwheeling to the surface in certain lights, subtly lost from it in others.

He finds Fanny in an upstairs room that smells of drafty wallpapered emptiness, her chin on the windowsill, chipping paint away with her thumbnail. Peels of paint lie on the sill and the floor. "Hey," he says. "You didn't swallow any of those, did you?"

She shakes her head, chin pivoting on the sill, her nose nearly touching glass. "I don't eat paint," she says, with dignity.

"I think about things like that, *chico*. I'm a father." He sits in a corner, deciding from her silence that she should have his entire attention. Since Christopher was born, he has too often felt he had nothing left over for Fanny – though he swore that would never happen. "So how are you?" he says. "How's school been?"

To his surprise, she pulls a folded slip of notebook paper from her pocket. "My teacher said I had to give you this."

"What is it?"

"I can't read writing yet. Only printing." She drops it to the floor.

He picks it up and begins to crease it into an airplane. Should he open the window and let it fly? "But you didn't like the idea of giving it to me?"

"I was going to. I was waiting."

He tucks the airplane into a pocket, walks to her on his knees, and waits for her to turn her head, but she doesn't; at arm's length, she is so still he can hear pigeons walking on the wooden shingles of the roof. "Tell me something, Fan," he pleads. "Have I seemed far away lately?"

"No."

"Because I want you to know you can always find me. Have you felt, maybe, that it's been hard to get my attention?"

"You're just you."

"Yes," he says, "but is that good or bad?" He pretends the end of her braid is a paintbrush and traces the corner of her mouth with it. "No answer, huh?" He tickles under her pale jaw until she has to smile. He says, "I can see you want me to fear the worst."

FANNY'S IN A LITTLE TROUBLE in school," Will tells his wife from the bedroom doorway. He has been prowling the lawn, as he does when he is uneasy, pulling up dandelions. Before marrying for the second time, he had tried to think it all through from Fanny's perspective, hoping to anticipate where the dangers for her would lie. He had come to the conclusion that there was another sort of risk, perhaps less immediately obvious, in her feeling that she had been responsible for keeping him from marrying again, and that in neither condition, married or unmarried, could he absolutely guarantee her safety. Yet he hates saying "Fanny's in a little trouble" so much that for an ominous moment he dislikes everything–past, present, and opalescent future; first wife, long gone, and second wife, regarding him sleepily; this house and the forlorn, mortgaged Victorian. In the bed, Carrie Ann wakes enough to turn her cheek to the baby's round forehead and direct her dark gaze, made darker by dilating pupils, at her husband, disliking him back in a rudimentary but very effective form of self-, and baby-, defense.

"She brought home a terrible note," Will says.

He rubs a knuckle against the door latch, meaning *Is this loose?*;

it is not. Carrie Ann, thrusting two fingers into the Pampers, smiles to find the powdered bottom dry. These simultaneous small discoveries dissolve the anxiety between them. Will continues to click the latch, but now simply for the sound it makes, and because he likes latches, locks, lintels, dowels, and bolts.

"Fanny in trouble?" Carrie Ann fits the tip of her pretty nose into Christopher's ear, and he opens his eyes and looks questioning. So often the mood of one is either a premonition or a minutely lagging echo of the mood of the other.

"Nothing too serious."

"But *something*."

"Something," he agrees, and is halted by the intentness of the baby's nearsighted stare. Carrie Ann cups the back of the baby's head so that he seems a bald, bewildered old man gazing at the doorway. He has no eyebrows. "You should see him from here," Will says. "He looks like Einstein thinking about ice cream."

Carrie Ann licks the nearly invisible down above the perfect, almost comically precise, ear. Then, alternating licks with shaping strokes for which she uses the inside of her wrist, she flattens the tufts at the crown of the head. A fist floats her way, opening into a starfish of sticky fingers, each of which she sucks in turn, causing – Will can see it, though she can't – the corners of the mouth to turn down in sober baby pleasure, the peak of the upper lip to glisten. Until the amniocentesis, Will had been frightened because he wanted the baby so badly yet believed in spite of himself that something would turn out to be wrong. He had urged the test on Carrie Ann, although she was thirty-two and her obstetrician didn't recommend amniocentesis until the woman was thirty-four. Will held her hand when, in the sonogram, the fetus appeared. He searched the screen for a fist, a foot, a tiny penis, but there was only the grainy, flickering C of the fetal back turned toward them. The baby oil that had aided in the conduction of the sound waves was washed from Carrie Ann's belly, the needle dived delicately in, delicately out, and the nurse said it was over.

Once they knew the baby was all right, and that it was a boy,

Carrie Ann mused through the rest of the pregnancy, talking to her belly, praising its kicks. What Will sometimes wonders is: Did the baby – or fetus – forgive him, and did he do something he ought to be forgiven for? He finds it interesting that the first question always precedes the second, and whenever he attempts to phrase them to himself in the more logical order they resist. They freeze exactly where they are.

Now when Will gets up in the night and pads down the hallway, the baby sometimes tries to nurse from his father's chest (is that forgiveness?), the corky nipple, hidden within a whorl of dark male hair, hardening helplessly as the hungry vacuum fastens upon it, and remaining there, stinging between the silky gums, until the baby exhales it with a sigh of disappointment. The baby's head makes a snug, familiar fit in Will's left hand, and he rocks Christopher close to his chest down the long unlit hall. Once, half asleep, he caught himself whispering, "It's me. It's me. Me," to the small face.

He was far too young, too unsure of himself, to be so available when Fanny was born. There is a little scene that unreels now and then in his mind: Fanny, her chin in her palm, telling her psychiatrist how distant her father was, how she could never seem to reach or please him, and her psychiatrist nodding gloomily. For some reason, Will finds this fable of the future reassuring. Perhaps it is because (at twenty? at nineteen?) Fanny is beautiful, or because psychiatry is his profession and she has turned to it, which would seem to imply she hasn't rejected him completely. It's not as if, in his mind's eye, she were without hope. So now he rattles the latch again and lets the note fall to the quilt. "You're not going to like it," he warns.

Dear Dr. and Mrs. Giles:

Ordinarily, we ask parents to come in so that things can be discussed face to face, but I know how busy you must be with the new baby. I am aware that a new baby in the household is a real test for everybody and that the natural tendency might be to leave a self-sufficient child like Fanny on her own more often, but my feeling is that something is worrying Fanny. She is such an achiever that her recent unwillingness to participate in class discussions, and her confusion when called on, really stand out. She has also been responsible for a series of small thefts. A paperweight belonging to another girl, and some other little things, were found in her coat pockets.

These things seem so unlike her they may be symptoms of some deeper problem, and I wondered if you'd agree to have Fanny talk to our school counselor, Mr. Yatsumoto?

Best wishes, and congratulations,
Delia Dorsey

"What a bitch," Carrie Ann says. "Delia Dorsey. What a funny mix of accusation and flattery this is. I think the entire letter is evidence of a truly small mind at work. I mean, it really depresses me to think that Fanny has fallen into her hands." Christopher mews for her breast. She rakes up her T-shirt and lets the breast descend. "She'll see Mr. Yatsumoto over my dead body."

"You know," Will says, "I thought the only thing wrong with moving was that Fanny would have to change schools."

"I hate this," Carrie Ann says, reading over the baby's head. "'Symptoms of some deeper problem.' If only someone like Delia Dorsey had been around to finger the young Richard Nixon, we'd never have had to go through Watergate and be disillusioned as a nation. She obviously doesn't know the first thing about Fanny. Do you want to know one reason I fell in love with you so fast? Because you were alone and yet you had this bright, serious, *serious* little girl, and I thought, He must be doing something right."

"Not anymore I'm not." Will lies down on the bed with the interesting sensation that he is trapping Carrie Ann, keeping her in place, because she is under the quilt and he is on it. The baby's head doesn't turn, though his temple pulses with the quick, small sucks that have drawn the nipple into his mouth. "I think I must be doing something pretty wrong. Haven't you noticed a change? Fanny's almost stopped confiding in me. That's never happened before."

Carrie Ann strokes his forehead and he smells baby on her

wrist. "Oh, Will. Maybe it was time for it to happen."

"I don't believe that."

"Some things are inevitable, but you don't believe that, either, do you?"

"I think believing that is a way of giving in."

"If I think about it too long, I'm going to get really furious at Delia Dorsey and Mr. Yatsumoto, and then my milk will stop."

He stands up, the mattress creaking. "I'm going," he says. "We can't have your milk stopping."

"Will?"

He is in the doorway. "What?"

"Now I feel guilty."

"Don't feel guilty," he says.

ON FANNY'S QUILT, pink with indigo stars of eight points each, Will turns on his side and sings into her hair,

> The fox went out on a dreary night
> And he prayed for the moon to give him light –

"Stop," Fanny says. "I don't like that anymore."

"You don't?" He pretends astonishment, thinking astonishment is what she wants, but really he is used to things changing fast. She has never been one for the same fairy tale night after night. "How about another song?"

"No."

"Want to read 'East of the Sun, West of the Moon'?"

"No. Dad?"

"Nnnnn-nh?" He *loves* her hair: fine, red-gold, kinky, the neat part white as bone and so sweet-smelling. Adult hair was never like that.

"How far is it from here to my house?" Fanny asks.

"Not so far." He remembers a story a patient told him – how the patient's daughter had been struck with grief because the family's battered old Volkswagen was about to be sold. "You mean you'd like to come back sometimes and see this place?"

"Can't I, if I want?"

"Look. This star on the quilt is the new house, see? Then you go around the corner, take the first left, go straight one, two, three blocks, then you turn right, like this" – he walks it with his fingers – "and bingo, there's our house. Does that seem too hard to remember?"

"No."

"Don't worry, you'll get it. You're a quick study, *chico*."

"I am?"

"Sure. It's a pleasure to tell you things, because you get them so fast."

"What happens if you're wrong?"

"If I'm wrong about what?" he says.

"What if I never really learned the things you were telling me? What if I forgot them all?"

"All? You wouldn't forget them all. Some knowledge you're born with. You have your mother's sense of direction." A rule long abided by: praise her mother to her as often as possible, in particular when praise is due. He points to the quilt. "This is the new house. You're here. Now you walk it."

She walks her fingers around the first corner, follows the pink for three blocks with a precision that almost kills him, and is getting warm when he catches her hand and swallows it to the knuckles, making devouring noises. "I forgot," he says around her fingers, "to warn you about the black hole in between. Mmmmmmm, nnnnnh, how good you are, delicious child, all gone."

To his astonishment, the gray eyes brim. He lets go of her hand. "What? Did that hurt?"

"No."

"I didn't think it was hard enough to hurt. Was it?"

"No."

"Are you worried about what the note said, then? Because I'm not."

"I know it."

"Then, Fanny?" She turns on her side, facing the wall, and he puts his cheek to her warm, small back. "Fanny?" Still no answer. "Fanny?"

At last she says, warily, "What?"

"Can't you tell me what's wrong?" He feels all his patience, professional and domestic, trained and intuitive, impartial and yearning, brought to the finest point of attention, his nose buried in the cotton flannel of her nightgown, his eyes closed, his heart hanging on her next word, which is:

"Nothing."

ON FRIDAY, after following Fanny through the new house, Will pretends he is blind and pats down the wall by the front door for the switch, missing it. A realtor, leading the way through one of the houses they considered, told him it takes nearly a month before you acquire that seemingly instinctive way of being able, in the dark, to put your hand directly on the light switch. The realtor seems to have been right. "Have you given any thought to where you'd like the telephone, Fan? The telephone guys are coming tomorrow, right in the middle of everything."

"Will you call?"

"Will I call?" Bemused, he locks the door behind them. She jumps to the railing, draws her knee to her chest and begins to rock strenuously. A neighbor's cat is in the corner of the porch.

"Fanny, I've told you about that. Stop."

"Will you call?" The neighbor's cat comes close; with her bare foot, toes extended, Fanny strokes the cat's head.

"From the clinic? I always call. You know that."

"You always used to."

"I don't get it, *chico*. Why's it going to be different?"

"What about," she says with an effort, "when I'm here, and they're there, then will you call me?"

"Who's they?"

"Carrie Ann," she says, "and the baby."

"So where are you, and where are they?"

"They're in your house," she says. "And I'm moved in here, tomorrow."

"Oh, *chico*," he says. "Is that what you think?"

She lets a foot rest lightly on the cat's head; delicately, with constraint, the cat licks its chest. "I know you have to have a house for just you and Carrie Ann and Christopher. I know you do. I like this house all right."

"Oh, Fan, no! Listen to me. It isn't that way at all. That was only a joke, the way I kept saying that this house was yours. This house is for *all* of us to live in – we're moving out of the old house together, into this one. We're a family. We're a little bigger family than before because of Christopher, but we would never want to live apart from you. Never. We couldn't stand it."

The cat hooks a paw as if to scratch at Fanny's ankle, and only swats – swift, small, apprehensive swats, claws in.

"I'm not sure about that cat, Fan."

"The cat won't hurt me." In proof, the cat begins to purr, and turns its cheek to Fanny's callused heel, buffing its head back and forth.

"Fanny?" he says. "It must have been so lonely for you."

"Forget it. Just forget it, Dad."

CARRIE ANN puts the tip of her nose into Christopher's ear. She closes her eyes and inhales. Very dexterously, in his sleep, his fist opens and closes, closes and opens, thumb over fingers, fingers over thumb, in a way that is both delightful and monotonous to watch closely, the fist surrounding, and never quite releasing, some strands of Carrie Ann's hair. She lifts her mouth to Will for his kiss. When she turns her head, the strands caught in the baby's fist draw tight.

"How could she think up something like that?" she says. "It would never even have occurred to me that we needed to be on guard against Fanny getting an idea like that. How could you have possibly known she'd come up with something so far-fetched?"

"It wasn't farfetched," he says. "It was reasonable, in its way. She was only listening to what I said."

She pats the quilt, signalling *Lie down;* he nods toward the hallway, meaning *I have to go talk to her some more.* Carrie Ann persists in patting the quilt: *I want to comfort you. Don't you need it, too?* So he does lie down, his body anchoring her body in place, and her foot, below the quilt, slides slowly down the length of his calf above it. She whispers, so she won't wake the baby, "God, Will, you want to know something? I think it's just about the saddest thing that's ever happened in the world, don't you?"

Will puts his head on her shoulder. The baby between them, they lie staring at the wide shadowed ceiling. She giggles, and suddenly they are both shaking with soft laughter, quite silent, something neither son nor daughter will ever hear.

SARA VOGAN

Sunday's No Name Band

JANEEN BROKE HER ARM at work, an industrial accident we call it. The men in the kitchen have been discussing Workman's Comp and lawsuits based on negligence. If she receives a windfall they think she should build a recording studio.

Janeen's the bass player in our band. Dana and I are going to give her a bath, her first since the accident on Monday. Dana's a nurse. She's also six months pregnant. She straddles the dirty clothes hamper in the corner of the bathroom, giving orders. I'm to perform the actual bathing and my heart knocks about my chest as I imagine Janeen slipping, the broken arm smacking against the tub tiles.

It's Sunday afternoon, raining like it does out here during the winter. Janeen's bath has become a party, mostly because none of us knows what to do with this Sunday afternoon without her. Usually we practice on Sundays in a storage area behind the shop where Janeen works. Matt, my husband and our rhythm guitar player, invited Dana, our vocalist, and her husband Chris who is our drummer. I invited Frank, our lead guitarist. I like things neat, as formal as classical piano, as precise as sheet music. Everyone's here, instead of in the practice space where we've spent each Sunday for the past eight months.

While Dana and Janeen and I are in the bathroom, Matt fusses over his beans and ham hocks in the kitchen on the other side of the wall. Frank and Chris say they will help him. We've decided to call this a Depression Chic dinner, enjoying the pun, trying to mask our disappointment with laughter.

"We should put the deck chair in the tub," Dana says. "That way she can sit down and you can work around her."

We agree this sounds like a good idea, so I go get the deck chair, but it won't fit. We settle for a stepladder which does. This doesn't leave much room to maneuver and my palms sweat as I place it in the tub.

Dana surveys the stepladder, the space heater for extra warmth. "A piece of cake."

"Then why don't you do it?" I say. "You're the professional here. I haven't even given my dog a bath in about two years." Again, I see Janeen falling, the broken arm smashing like glass.

"I do this for a living. Trust me. You'll do fine." She rubs her belly. "Besides, I'm not sure I'd fit." She eases herself back on the clothes hamper, as round and imperturbable as a Buddha. She laughs, but I see nothing funny here.

Janeen looks apprehensively at the tub. "I think if I keep a grip on my elbow you can get everything but the arm pits." The break is too near the shoulder to cast, held in place with an elastic bandage. I'm afraid when she undresses the arm will dangle like something in a horror movie.

I adjust the space heater, directing the flow of warm air. Dana rises from her seat to help Janeen undress. The doctor put the webbing of bandage around Janeen's waist and over her shoulder, where her guitar strap usually sits. Her bass always reminds me of a black lacquer woman she holds in her arms. She keeps a red pick stuck in the facing like a heart.

Dana and Janeen struggle with her boots. "It was so easy to get into them," she moans. Bending is difficult for Janeen, as it is for Dana with her baby. Janeen looks close to tears. "I never imagined it would be so tough getting them off." She stares at the ceiling, studying it. Perhaps she's in pain. "I can't comb my hair. I can't open a carton of milk."

I could get Janeen's boots off in two seconds, but I let Dana work with them. It's good to see Dana in motion, active. A curious light has come over Dana these days, as if her pregnancy wasn't something she carried with her daily, but a new idea crossing her mind fresh and different each time. She often misses what's said in conversations, her cues in the music when she's supposed to sing. This will be Dana's first baby and her fourth pregnancy. The baby is due the same week Dana turns 36.

"Brushing my teeth takes ten minutes. The toothbrush keeps falling over when I try to put the paste on it."

"We have a patient with all the fingers of his right hand, even his thumb, gone. He says he can do everything but hammer a nail." Dana begins to unfasten the bandage. I watch how her hands work in concert, one guiding the bandage, the other holding the ball.

Janeen's eyes look wild in the corners. "I don't want to make a career of this."

"Industrial accident," Dana says. "A slicing machine. There you go." She surveys Janeen's naked body, appraising her work. She smooths her palms on her stomach again and returns to her seat on the clothes hamper.

I hover around Janeen as she steps over the rim of the tub and eases herself down on the stepladder. "OK?" I ask, although I can see she's fine.

"I want a towel," she says, "to cover my face. I don't want my makeup to run. It took me all morning, one handed."

I can't imagine taking a shower with makeup on. I never suspected Janeen wore it. I study her face and see how carefully it's done, the fine peach bloom on her cheeks, the dark lashes. Janeen's always been admired for her fine coloring and intense eyes. It startles me to realize the effect of her face is artificial.

Out in the kitchen, on the other side of the wall, we hear something crash, then the deep laughter of men. We look at each other, the way women do. Men in the kitchen. We know what to expect. "I'm glad it's not my house," Dana says.

"Here comes the water." I reach for the taps. Janeen ducks her face into the towel, her back to the shower nozzle. Stripping out of my clothes, I hand them to Dana, who drops them in a pile at her feet. I step into the shower, right under the stream of hot water. It pumps against the back of my neck, spraying over my shoulders, warm and relaxing. Gently, as if her skull were broken instead of her arm, I begin to massage shampoo into Janeen's hair. The arm is a bright blue bruise and looks contagious, as if it could spread across her back, her scalp. As if I could catch it on my hands.

Janeen can't drive, bathe herself, open a can. I feel her defeat. She won't be able to play for at least two months. I know in her mind the band has already dissolved. Dana and Chris will lose interest with the baby so close. Frank will drift off, much the way he drifted in. Matt and I will find something else to do on Sunday afternoons. All of us are too old for rock and roll bands. Those golden days we keep striving for are now fifteen years behind us. We get together on Sundays because we all missed the same lessons. We play other people's tunes, the blues and rock and roll we grew up with and remember more clearly than lullabys.

What kind of band was it, anyhow? We're a band without a name and none of our own songs. We've never even played a gig. We settled into our lives with only Sundays to spare for music, a few hours when we can remember a time when we all felt young and bright and full of promise. A two-month hiatus will be as physical as the break in Janeen's arm.

The shower curtain opens and Dana steps in, on the other side of Janeen's body. She has a bar of soap and begins to expertly work it around Janeen's breasts. Dana hums, her belly bobbing above Janeen's knees. Janeen sits as still as a fixture while Dana's hands dart among crevices, tucking bits of lather into the curves.

But Dana isn't humming. She's singing, soft and low in that sweet voice of hers, a voice that can stay on pitch. I know right away what it is, as if I picked it up from the rhythm of the water beating on my back.

"Well, they call it Stormy Monday,
But Tuesday's just as bad."

I look up across Janeen. Dana's right, of course, I join her, imagining Billie Holiday and her gardenia, the smoky clubs of Harlem. I hear the riffs I would do on the piano and my fingers begin to chord on Janeen's head. The rush of the water makes us sound better than we actually are, adding the beat like Chris's drums and fills. The tile of the tub acts as an echo chamber and the song becomes as thick as the steam rising all around us. "Wednesday's worse, and Thursday's all so sad." We sing from deep in our diaphragms, watching each other's faces so we don't take a breath at the same moment. Janeen straightens. Her face comes out of the towel and she joins us on the next verse.

"The eagle flies on Friday,
And Saturday I go out to play."

We are all naked and wet and yet for the first time I can really see us standing before strangers, our instruments ringing with sound, our voices rising with a passion no practice session can provide. We will wear gardenias in our hair, dresses cut to show off our shoulders. I imagine Matt in a tuxedo, Dana with a waist again. Janeen and Frank will resume their affair and smile at each other the way they used to when we first began this band. We will all be dreaming in the dark and our eyes will meet the light and be blinded with the power of the song.

"Lord, please have mercy on me, please have mercy on me." Janeen swivels her head, back and forth between us, smiling. Water sprays over her face and little runs of makeup trickle down her cheeks like beads of sweat. Janeen sings, and sings. I've never seen this smile on her face before. I consider asking if I could wash off her makeup, but I know, as close as we are in the tub right now, we are not close enough for that.

We belt out a rousing finale. "Lord, send my baby back home to me!" And we laugh, giggling like girls in junior high. Dana puts her hands on the small of her back and stretches, her belly ballooning in front of her. Shampoo and soap fleck the tile walls, the shower curtain. Steam swirls around us, creating thermals that disappear some place near the ceiling. You can't keep your eye on them, no matter how hard you try.

Janeen laughs. "I feel better." She runs her good hand across her cheek, wiping at the ruined makeup.

The water begins to turn coolish. It will be cold in another few minutes. "You'll have to stand for the rinse," I say. Immediately I'm sorry I've done this. Janeen's face falls out of the smile. Dana has that distracted look again. But we can't stay in the shower all afternoon, ice water beating on our backs. Yet for a moment, that's what we imagined, that somehow if we stayed here long enough we could all come out healed.

Janeen stands and Dana steps out of the tub. I grab the stepladder and follow, feeling the chill of the air in spite of the space heater. Through the curtain we can watch Janeen turn herself slowly under the shower nozzle, washing off soap, shampoo, her makeup.

I reach into the tub and turn off the faucets. From the other room we hear noise. Men in the kitchen, Matt and Frank and Chris. They're singing. We watch each other's faces, catching the glint of laughter in our eyes, amazed, as if we are the only ones to have the privilege of singing on this Sunday afternoon. Dana takes a towel and covers Janeen, daubing at the water running off her onto the bathroom floor. I open the door and the song is clearer.

"I can't get no
Satisfaction!
I can't get no
Girl reaction."

Dana's professional hands dry the injured arm. Our heads bob with the beat, our feet tapping time. We wait until the chorus before we join the song.

"But I try, and I try, and I try, and I try.
I can't get no (DaDaDum) Satisfaction!"

There's a round of applause from the kitchen. Someone, probably Matt, bangs on a pan. We will eat. Maybe Frank will offer to take Janeen home, the way he used to. Perhaps some day we will play in front of strangers. Maybe there won't be gardenias or tuxedos, but the lights will blind us and the songs will rise.

"Saved again by the Rolling Stones," Janeen says.

Saved again, indeed. We know all the little pieces connecting us to our private pasts. We are learning the moments, like singing in the shower, that will connect us long after Janeen's arm heals, Dana's baby is born.

The steam in the bathroom disappears. One minute you can hold it with your eyes, the next you're staring at empty air. It's the same feeling you have when a song is over, the tune hanging on in your mind.

BOBBIE ANN MASON

Blue Country

THE BLUE LANTERN INN – that's a name straight out of a Nancy Drew book," said Nancy Culpepper.

"Is Nancy Drew your namesake?" teased Jack Cleveland, Nancy's husband.

Nancy laughed. "Nancy Drew always stopped at some quaint wayside inn for tea, and there would be a mystery to solve. The inns were just like this. I feel I've been here before."

Nancy and Jack were at the Blue Lantern Inn on the coast above Boston. They had come for the weekend to attend the wedding of a friend from graduate school who was finally getting married to the man she had lived with for five years. Nancy and Jack had driven for six hours from Pennsylvania. On the way Jack had said, "Why couldn't the wedding be two weeks from now, when the autumn leaves are just right?" They used to live in New England, and Jack was crazy about the fall foliage. He was always critical of autumn in Pennsylvania. He would complain about the brown-and-gold splendor on the mountain ridge near their home. Not a single flaming red sugar maple on the whole mountain, he would point out, like someone judging a parade.

That evening, in a seafood house on a wharf, Jack and Nancy ripped apart bright lobsters and laughed. They drank a bottle of rosé – to match the lobster, Jack said. But the colors didn't match at all. Jack acted silly, calling her "Toots," the way he did to tease her when they were first married. Nancy called him "Mr. Toots" in return and giggled. Jack had been teasing her all day. Going to a wedding made them happy. Water leaked from the boiled lobster into Nancy's lap. Jack splintered a claw and a tender orange hand slithered out.

Afterward, they walked in the dark on the beach in front of the Blue Lantern Inn. The tide had gone so far out they had to hike to meet it. The sand was wet and marshy in places, and it was too dark to see the water. Some birds skittered by quietly.

"I had forgotten how much I love the ocean," Jack said. "I can't wait till Sunday."

"I'm not sure I want to go out there in a little boat to watch whales," Nancy said. "The idea is terrifying."

"It won't be terrifying in the daytime," Jack said. "Whales are friendly."

"But they're so big."

"They're like horses. Horses are very careful not to step on cats and chickens."

"Tell that to Ahab," said Nancy, squeezing his hand.

In the inn during the night, she heard the sea whispering, and toward morning she heard a gurgling sound – rain falling from the drain spouts. Suddenly, there was a sharp tapping on the door and an urgent voice: "Phone call. Phone call." Nancy was in her jeans and sweat shirt and downstairs in the lobby before she could realize what she had heard. She was afraid something had happened to their child, Robert, who was staying with friends at home.

It was Nancy's mother, in Kentucky. "Nancy? Did I get you up? Granny passed away last night, about eleven o'clock."

Nancy had expected this phone call for years. But now she was stunned and her mother sounded bewildered. Nancy's grandmother was ninety-four and had been arthritic and senile for several years. During the past summer her health had deteriorated, and for many months Nancy had not traveled without notifying her parents where to reach her.

Nancy's mother said, "She had mass-matter on the brain."

"What in the world is mass-matter on the brain?" Nancy cried. A tall man in a blue blazer turned his head in her direction.

Mother said, "Sometimes the blood vessels running to your brain mat together in a pocket? They call it mass-matter."

"You mean she had a stroke."

"She was acting wild on us all day," Mother went on. "Hollering and carrying on. Trying to walk for the first time in a year. I went in about ten-thirty to give her a pill and I thought she was dead. But she wasn't completely dead yet."

While her mother described the funeral plans, Nancy looked out the front window and saw that the ocean was still far away. The tide had come in and gone out again. She should leave for Kentucky immediately, for the funeral was the next day.

"I don't know how soon I can get there," she said. "I'll have to check with the airlines." She suddenly looked down, wondering if she had remembered to dress. Guests were entering the dining room for breakfast.

She spoke with her father, who sounded weary and distant.

"Can't you wait till Monday?" Nancy asked him.

"Nobody would come on Monday. They'd have to work."

"I'll try to get there," she said. "I just woke up. I'm looking out at the sea. It's beautiful. We're at this nice inn – "

"I know how much you always cared for Granny, and you had always planned to come back for her funeral," said Daddy.

"Yes," Nancy said.

Jack was still sleeping. Telephone calls never alarmed him. Nancy instinctively feared bad news from the telephone. She was fourteen, on the farm in Kentucky, when the family first got a telephone, the same year they got television. Jack came from a different world – private school, summer camps. How did we ever get together? Nancy thought wildly, as she woke him up and told him the news.

"Granny had some kind of fit," she said. "It sounded unreal." She remembered the way her grandmother lay curled up, barely able to turn, for so long. Nancy's father had once said, "Old people get that way, drawed up like a baby in the womb." They had attempted once to take her to a nursing home, but she had refused to go.

Jack sat up on his elbows, looking disappointed. Jack, a photographer, had planned to make a wedding album for Laurie and Ed as a present.

"Do you want me to fly down with you?" he asked.

"No. It's not necessary." Jack was always uncomfortable in the South. The first time he went with her, in the late sixties, a truck driver had threatened to beat him up. It was Jack's hair. Nancy said now, "You don't have to go. I don't want you to miss the wedding, and you were counting on seeing whales tomorrow."

"You may not even be able to get there because of the airline strike," Jack said, getting out of bed and parting the curtains. "Oh, it's raining," he said. "I was going to run."

"Well, if I can't get there, then I can't get there," said Nancy.

"How would they feel if you didn't go?"

"I don't know." She pulled her sweat shirt over her head. Her face was still in her sweat shirt when Jack drew her to him and held her, waiting for her to cry.

"Would you call the airlines for me while I take a shower?" Nancy asked. "This hasn't registered yet. Look at me. I'm not even crying."

In the shower, Nancy realized that everything in the Blue Lantern Inn was blue. The wallpaper was blue. The rugs were blue. In the lobby downstairs, seashells on blue tiles were mounted on the wall. The inn seemed to be the ideal place she had aspired toward since her childhood, when she read about the pleasant, cozy tearooms in the storybooks. She tried to picture her grandmother's face – the gentle woman she loved – but all she could see was a silhouette of an old woman hunched over her dishpan set on the gas stove to heat. In the stove, in a compartment next to the oven, would be food from dinner saved for supper. Miraculously, no one in the family had ever had food poisoning. Nancy pushed open the clouded-glass window in the shower and saw the ocean beating, gray in the rain. She dreaded the thought of flying in the rain.

"The only plane that will get you to Louisville with decent connections leaves Boston in two hours," Jack told Nancy when she came out of the shower. "And you'll have to fly standby. There's one from New York at six, but we'd have to drive to New York, and there's nothing out of Louisville until noon tomorrow. I don't think that one would get you home in time for the funeral. Anyway, all the flights are booked solid, and you'd have to take a chance on getting a seat."

"Let's eat and think about this," said Nancy. She had hoped for an evening flight so she would not have to miss the wedding. It occurred to her that Jack would have to drive back to Pennsylvania alone.

"What are you feeling?" he asked.

"I don't know." She spread cold lotion on her legs. "I feel inconvenienced," she said. "I mean, it doesn't seem personal. She was so old."

Jack said, "I hope you're relieved, Nancy. She's been a terrible strain on your parents."

"I know it," Nancy said, pulling on corduroy slacks. "She's driven my mother crazy. If I cry, it will be for my mother."

"Maybe you should wait and go down in a week or two and spend some time with your parents. They might need you more then."

"That might be better – and I have that important meeting at work on Tuesday." Nancy began to relax. Jack was always so clearheaded. She put on an Icelandic wool sweater she had bought in Scotland once when she and Jack went looking for the Loch Ness monster. Jack called the sweater her "sheep."

"Why *don't* you go down later?" he said, looking happier. He did a few deep knee bends.

Nancy gazed at snapshots of previous guests on a bulletin board in the dining room. On a paper plate thumbtacked next to the tide tables, someone had scrawled, YES, THE MOONIES

ARE HERE. A smiling gray-haired man in a striped sweater said to Jack, "We come here every year. We were here all week and the weather was *glorious* until today."

"There's an artists' colony here as good as on the Cape," a short woman, his wife, said, beaming.

Nancy took orange juice, coffee, and a blueberry muffin from a sideboard and sat at the corner of the long table, facing the ocean. Jack sat down and handed her a napkin and silverware. "You forgot these," he said gently. He chatted with the cheerful couple while Nancy ate and gazed out the window at the vacant sky and water. Her appetite surprised her. The muffins were homemade, according to the other guests.

Jack brought Nancy another muffin. "Are you okay?" he asked.

"I think so."

"Do you know what you want to do?"

"I don't want to travel in the rain." She spread butter on the muffin and watched it crumble. She said, "When my parents were young, they wanted to build a house of their own half a mile down the road. They wanted to buy a piece of land and build. Instead, they built that house next door, on Granddaddy's land. Mother remembers how Granny fretted at the idea of Daddy moving half a mile away. She said, 'Well, what if he was to get sick? Who would take care of him?' She didn't want her precious son out of her sight and didn't trust my mother to look out for him. Mother bore that insult to this day. And *she* ended up taking care of Granny all those years."

"Think of how free your parents are going to be now," Jack said.

Nancy ate a bite of muffin. "I know I should go," she said slowly. "But it seems to me that if you have a choice between a wedding and a funeral, you should go to the wedding."

"It's up to you."

"I know you want to take pictures, and we drove so far."

More guests were entering the dining room, talking about the weather.

Nancy said to Jack, "Later I'll double-check and see if there's some way I could get there late tonight or tomorrow morning. And I'll call home later today. They'll be at the funeral home all afternoon anyway."

Suddenly, a small blond dog rushed into the dining room, followed by the woman who ran the guesthouse. She cried, "Tuffie – get back here! You know you're not supposed to be in Blue Country!"

The gray-haired man said to her, "It's too bad you have to live in the back of the house, without this beautiful view."

"Oh, in the winter we always move into Blue Country," she said, smiling and scooping up the dog from the blue rug. She tugged the dog's ribboned topknot. "Bad boy, Tuffie."

"That dog doesn't look half as guilty as I do," Nancy said to Jack.

THE WEDDING had been planned for the beach, but because of the rain it was moved to a summer camp nearby. The redwood cottages, with elaborately carved cornices and red-painted trim, resembled a Russian peasant village. "Everything in New England is quaint," said Nancy as Jack's umbrella exploded into shape. They could hear the ocean roaring beyond a low, tree-lined hill. The clouds were rushing by, like something chased, so near they looked transparent as smoke.

The art studio, where the crowd was gathering, was unfinished inside, and spider plants dangled from two-by-fours braced together overhead. Some stretched canvases faced the wall, and the floor was paint-splotched. Nancy sat in a folding chair and scanned the crowd for familiar faces while Jack began photographing Laurie and Ed, who were already there. Nancy had not seen Laurie in four years, and they had met Ed only once, at a restaurant in Philadelphia when he was attending a computer conference. Someone was adjusting the flowers in Laurie's hair. Nancy did not remember ever seeing Laurie in a dress. Laurie kept hitching up her waistband. Ed, in a dark tuxedo with red, embroidered lapels, was greeting friends and smiling broadly.

Nancy remembered that at the restaurant in Philadelphia he had ordered baby octopus and that it had arrived intact, on a bed of pasta. Jack, who found Ed somewhat pretentious, had thought it was vulgar to order such a thing, but Nancy thought it had been adventurous.

When the musicians – two guitarists and a violinist – began playing, Nancy recognized Gypsy music in the wail of the violin. She recalled a Nancy Drew mystery involving Gypsies. She used to read those books on Granny's front porch. She sat on the porch swing, swinging as high as she could go and wishing hard that she could go someplace Nancy Drew went, and she begged Granny to run away with her, but Granny warned her against Gypsies and did not have a high opinion of unknown places. The violin was mournful at first, then sweet, then ecstatic, before shivering and retreating into a low moan.

Jack sat down beside Nancy. "I think I got some good shots," he said. "Doesn't Laurie look incredible?"

Two tall men walked with Laurie and Ed to the front of the room. One of the men took a white gown from his briefcase and fluffed it up. He threw it up in the air like pizza dough and caught it, then pulled it over his head. The other man, a rabbi, draped an embroidered vestment around his shoulders. Laurie tugged at her skirt.

"The minister must be a friend of theirs," said the woman sitting next to Nancy.

The rabbi spoke in Hebrew and offered Laurie and Ed a glass of wine. Suddenly, in the front row, a man stood up and began talking to Laurie. She turned to listen. Then he faced the audience and said apologetically, "I couldn't give Laurie away, because I don't own her. But I ran across some things last week that I wanted to share on this occasion." He thumbed through the papers in his hand, explaining that they were report cards and drawings he had saved from Laurie's childhood. "I have this Valentine here," he said. "It's signed, 'Love, Laurie.'" He cried, and Laurie, looking embarrassed, embraced him. When he sat down, a woman next to him stood up, her back to the audience, and read a poem titled "The Outermost Limits." Nancy saw the rain splatter the stained glass, and somewhere a baby cried. The rabbi raised a glass of wine and sang. Laurie and Ed took turns reading parts of their marriage contract. Laurie had a theatrical voice; she was an actress and had once had a part in a soap opera.

She read, "We join together in the bond of marriage, but we do so in protest against the established institution of marriage, an institution that enslaves women by making them property, thus denying them economic equality. We also protest against laws that prevent homosexual couples from marrying. Yet we join together, formally, in this bond, as an affirmation of the love that individual human beings can feel for one another."

Suddenly, Laurie and Ed were stomping on wine glasses wrapped in cloth napkins, and then with a cry of relief that the glasses broke successfully, they virtually leaped into each other's arms. The Gypsy music began. Nancy was crying, at last.

AT THE RECEPTION in the cafeteria, she found a price tag dangling on a nylon thread inside the cuff of her silk blouse. Jack bit it off, discreetly, and she pulled out the end of the thread.

"Minnie Pearl," he teased. Nancy smiled nervously. Umbrellas drifted past the windows. The stained glass over the doorway was an abstract design – broken lines like shattered glass.

During the day, while Jack took more pictures, and the people milled around her, Nancy forgot for indeterminate stretches of time the news from home. When it occurred to her, rushing forward in a little replay of the conversation with her mother, she still felt awkward, almost puzzled. The rain was pounding harder outside, and the hum of voices blended with it. Everyone seemed happy. Two older women were thrilled to learn that Nancy lived in Pennsylvania. One of them cried, "Oh, we go to Pennsylvania! Once a year we go down to New Hope, and sometimes at midnight our friends take us across the state line to play Midnight Beano."

"It's lots of fun!" said her companion, who had red lipstick smeared around her lips.

"And then after that they take us shopping at a discount store there." The woman grasped Nancy's arm and said, "It was such a lovely ceremony, especially when Laurie's father made that little speech."

"That was touching," said the other woman. "I clean for Laurie. Ed has allergies and can't stand a speck of dust."

"That poem was odd, though. Wasn't it odd?"

"Ed is very sensitive."

Nancy found Jack changing a lens. "The lighting's wrong," he said. "I need my bright lights. Look at all the shadows."

"It's appropriate, though, for the weather today," said Nancy, seeing the shadows, the jewel-light of the stained glass. The people, dressed for the autumn beach in wool and corduroy, looked like faded autumn leaves. She said, "I just talked to some women who go to New Jersey to play Midnight Beano, and then afterward they go discount shopping – in the middle of the night! Can you imagine! They were delightful."

"You seem to be enjoying yourself," Jack said.

"Should I?"

"Sure. It's a wedding."

"It's a wonderful wedding."

"Did you notice that there were two wine glasses?" asked Jack. "Laurie broke one too. Traditionally, only the man breaks a wine glass. It symbolizes the breaking of the hymen."

"Then what's the second glass supposed to mean – castration?"

Nancy and Jack were laughing the way they had the previous day.

They ate at a table with Karen Bordon, an acquaintance from graduate school. Nancy barely remembered her, but Karen said Nancy had once given her a ride to Pittsfield. Karen operated a camera for a Boston television station. She called herself a camera person. The man she was with, Malcolm, worked in color processing, and Jack and Malcolm and Karen talked in technicalities about film while Nancy concentrated on the food, which had been catered by a Beacon Hill restaurant Nancy and Jack used to go to. There was food at funerals too, Nancy thought. The neighbors would bring hams and pies and cakes.

Later, Nancy telephoned the airlines, rechecking the schedule. There were still no seats available, and now flights were being canceled because of the weather.

Nancy sat with the telephone in front of a window. She saw Jack out on the beach with his camera, aiming at the foggy scene. She imagined gray, empty space in the pictures.

On the telephone, Nancy's father didn't protest when Nancy explained the difficulty of the travel schedule. She promised to come down later to help them get adjusted and to help her mother clean out Granny's room.

Nancy repeated to her mother, "The airline schedules are erratic because of the strike. I wish you'd put it off till Monday."

"We'll get a better crowd on Sunday. We'll just have a handful anyway. Everybody her age has died off. All the pallbearers on her list are dead, or else they're down in their back. Remember that list she used to keep under her pillow? Oh, I wish you could see her! She's beautiful, the way they've got her fixed up. She told your daddy she didn't want an open casket – she didn't want people to see her looking so pitiful. But she'd be proud if she could see herself. Those big flower sprays you put on top of the casket have gone up, so we couldn't afford a big one. They cost about a hundred dollars, so we got the small one for fifty. If we'd had a closed casket with just that little spray on it – why that would look tooty!"

Nancy's mother talked on, describing the expenses of the funeral, the arrangements, the relatives who had called. Nancy let her mother talk. Jack was still out on the beach, oblivious to the chill wind. The water dashed against clay-colored rocks that had been cracked into hundreds of slices by a powerful force, probably glaciers. The slices had not separated. They made Nancy think of Droste chocolate oranges, which fall apart into perfect slices when tapped on the top.

Mother said, "She's just beautiful – she looks thirty years younger! Her hair's fixed nice, and I bought her a pretty blue dress, a dress like she would have liked, with a Peter Pan collar and tucks."

"I thought she had a blue dress she'd been saving."

"Well, it was out of style, and they had these dresses at the funeral home, so I bought one, and bought beads. She always liked jewelry. And she has a corsage, and inside the casket lid is a blue spray. I hope somebody brings a camera. I want to get some pictures for you. She didn't want all that money spent on her, but it was *her* money, and I'm spending it on *her*, to send her out in style."

"Are you going to be all right, Mom?" asked Nancy.

"Well, they say you're never prepared for anybody to die. And it's true."

Nancy shifted the receiver to her other ear. She said, "Your life is going to be different from now on. You and Daddy can go somewhere together for the first time in years. You can come and visit me – at last."

"This morning he told me something that floored me," Mother said. "He said, 'Do you realize that last night was the first night we slept in a house alone together in forty years?' I said no, but it's true. Forty years! There was always somebody here to take care of. Oh, you should see all the food the neighbors brought."

Nancy's mother described the food – ham, chicken, steak patties, three pies, two cakes, baked beans, three-bean salad, Jello salads. As she listened, Nancy kept her eyes on Jack out on the fractured rocks, a frail silhouette against the sea.

BACK AT THE RECEPTION, when Nancy finally cornered her old friend Laurie, who had once lived in a basement apartment below Nancy's and played Doors albums full blast, she felt glad she had stayed. Laurie's freckles danced around her smile.

"I've had so much champagne," she said. "And I've barely seen Ed since the ceremony. Is this what marriage is like?"

"It's a lovely wedding," said Nancy.

"Jack was so sweet to take those pictures."

"Are you going on a trip?"

"No. We took our honeymoon last week. But next week I'm going to Mexico with my brother. He's an archæologist, and I have this fabulous chance to go on a dig. Ed can't go because he has to work."

Nancy felt like confiding in Laurie, the way she used to when they studied together for exams. She found herself blurting out the news about her grandmother. It seemed improper to mar the wedding, and when Laurie made sympathetic remarks, Nancy said hastily, "It was expected. And she was old as Methuselah."

"It feels strange not going home, but I'm glad I'm here," she added. "And I'm glad you're doing something affirmative."

"That's the way we looked at it," Laurie said. "Ed's best friend died this summer, and that led to our decision to get married. We realized how little time there is."

Laurie was holding Nancy's hand. Her flowers were askew.

Nancy said, "I'm sure my mother will flip out when it hits her that she's free at last. They've been tied down on the farm for *years*, taking care of my grandmother. They've never even left Kentucky to visit me."

"Did you say your grandmother was your dad's mother?"

"Yes."

Laurie said, "If Ed's dad were to die and his mother had to move in with us, I'd divorce him in a minute. I wouldn't take care of my mother-in-law like that. I'm not even sure I could do it for my own mother." Laurie was looking around cautiously as she spoke. Her mother-in-law was eating cake on the far side of the room, and her mother was out of sight.

"Do you know what my mother said on the phone?" Nancy said. "She said last night was the first night in forty years that she and my father had spent alone together."

Laurie's look of astonishment pleased Nancy. It was the best gesture of sympathy: to be amazed.

ARE YOU OKAY, Nancy?" It was Jack, standing close, touching her. "You look off-balance."

"It's the champagne. I was okay until Mother started talking about how pretty Granny looked and telling about the dress. Now all I can think is this doll shut in a box in the ground with flowers in her face."

"You're not supposed to think about things like that."

"They really expected me to come home."

"I'm sorry I urged you not to go," Jack said.

Nancy drank some more champagne. "I couldn't go anyway in the fog," she said.

"You can go to Kentucky next week," Jack said.

"Yes. Oh, look! The musicians are packing up. I wish they wouldn't go. I loved that Gypsy violin."

ON SUNDAY the ocean was calm and the sky was a transparent blue, reflecting in the water. Nancy and Jack were on a sightseeing boat, heading out from shore. About five times Jack said he wished Robert was along. When he saw whales on TV, Robert would yell out with breathless excitement. Nancy kept thinking of the time her mother mentioned in a letter a traveling exhibition that had come to the shopping center – a whale in a tank in a trailer truck. The whale couldn't even turn around.

"What do you feel?" Jack asked her as the shore disappeared.

"Confused," said Nancy, looking forward to the horizon. A barge lay in line with it.

"You've got to get your mom and dad up to visit us."

"Somehow I can't picture it. It would freak them out. They never went anywhere. I was the one who left, but they always expected me to keep running back."

The boat was passing close to a buoy, bobbing casually on the water. A seabird landed on it, like a spacecraft docking.

"They sent me out as an explorer," Nancy said. "Like Columbus."

"I read that Columbus brought syphilis back to Europe."

"That's what happens when you go out adventuring," Nancy said. "It's the nature of the game."

Jack tied the drawstring of her hood under her chin. She said, "I didn't wear my watch because I didn't want to get it wet. Do you have your pocket calculator?"

Jack patted his breast pocket and nodded.

"I want you to tell me when it's three o'clock," she said. "The funeral's at two. That's three, Eastern time. I want to know when it is, so I can think about it happening. At least I can be there in my imagination."

Jack punched tiny buttons on his calculator so that a beeper would sound at three. "I'm sorry I urged you not to go to Kentucky," he said. "It was selfish."

"No, I keep telling you, it's okay."

"If I die, I don't want you to make a fuss. You can just throw me in the ocean."

Nancy could almost see Granny's face. The last time Nancy saw her, she had taken a kitten in to show her. On TV reports about pet therapy, children took puppies and kittens into nursing homes for old people to pet. Nancy had a vivid memory of an old woman's chalky face lighting up when she held a puppy in her lap. Nancy had offered the kitten to her grandmother, but Granny wouldn't touch it. Her face was grim and selfish. She didn't want the curtains opened either, and she didn't want a radio. No one read to her. Staring at the ocean, Nancy thought that its vast blankness and mystery were like her grandmother's mind in those final months – something private and deep she had saved for herself.

"Whale ahoy!" the captain cried suddenly.

Nancy did not pay attention when three o'clock came, for they were among the whales. A whale's back appeared like a large boulder out in the water, and then three or four, like stepping stones. As the boat drew nearer, a whale leaped up like a jack-in-the-box. The passengers were shouting and clumsily aiming their cameras. Water smacked their faces, and Jack and Nancy gasped with laughter, as though laughter could protect them. The whales began moving, making deep swirls and waves in the water, and then a humpback whale, barnacled like a circus elephant decorated with sequins, rose completely out of the water and seemed to fly. At that moment Nancy knew that this – not something quaint or cozy – was what she had come so far away from home to see. The engine stopped, and the boat started to rock in the wake of the whales. Jack's face was insane with delight. His camera hung loose on his chest. Another whale breached, close by, with a force that shot water up to the sky. As it plunged downward, its tail flukes wiggled, like an airplane tipping its wings as a signal to someone below.

TESS GALLAGHER

Bad Company

THE WIDOW DROVE into the cemetery, parked near the mausoleum, and got out with her flowers. The next day was Memorial Day, and the cemetery would be thronged with people. Entire families would arrive to bring flowers to the graves of their loved ones. Tiny American flags would decorate the graves of the veterans. But today the cemetery was still and deserted.

When she reached her husband's grave she saw that someone had been there before her. The little metal vase affixed to the headstone was crammed with daffodils and dandelions. But whoever had put them there hadn't known the difference between a flower and a weed. She put her flowers down on the flat gravestone and stared at the unsightly wad of flowers. Only a man could have thrown together such a bouquet, she thought.

She raised her hand to her brow and looked around. A short distance away she saw a girl stretched out next to a grave. She hadn't seen her at first because the girl had not been standing. The girl lay propped on one elbow so she could look down at the gravestone next to her. When the widow walked toward her, the girl did not lift her head or move. Then the widow saw her pluck a blade of grass and touch it to her lips before she let it fall. The widow's shadow fell across the girl, and the girl looked up.

"Did you happen to see anyone at that grave over yonder?" the widow asked.

The girl raised herself into a sitting position. She looked at the widow but didn't say anything.

She's crazy, the widow thought, or else she can't talk. She regretted having spoken to the girl at all. Then the girl stood up and touched her hands together.

"There was a man. About an hour ago," the girl said. "He could of been to that grave."

"It's my husband," the widow said. "His grave. But I don't know who could have left those flowers."

The widow noticed that the grave next to the girl had no flowers. She wondered at this, that anyone would come to a grave and then leave nothing behind. At this time of day the shadows of the evergreens at the near end of the graveyard crept gradually across the grass. It sent a chill through her shoulders. She drew her sweater together at the neck and folded her arms.

"He didn't stay long," the girl volunteered. And then she smiled. The widow thought it was a nice thing after all to speak to this stranger and to be answered courteously in this sorrowful place.

"He was over at the mausoleum too," the girl said.

The widow thought hard who it might be. She only knew one person buried in the mausoleum. He had been dead ten years now and only one member of his family still survived.

"It must have been Lloyd Medly," the widow said. "His brother, Homer, is over there in the mausoleum. His ashes, anyway. They grew up with my husband and me, those boys." The widow had spoken to Lloyd just last week on the telephone. He was in the habit of calling up every few weeks to see how she was. "Homer's on my mind a lot," he'd said to her when they last talked.

"I don't know anybody in the mausoleum," the girl said. The widow looked down and saw a little white cross engraved over the name on the stone. There were some military designations she didn't understand and, below the name, the dates 1914-1967.

"Nineteen-fourteen! That's the year I was born," the widow said, as if surprised that anyone born in that year had already passed on. For a moment it seemed as if she and the one lying there in the ground had briefly touched lives.

"I can barely remember him," the girl said. "But when I stay here a while, things come back to me." She was a pretty girl with high Indian cheekbones. The widow noticed the way her hips went straight down from her waist. She had slow, black eyes, and the widow guessed her to be in her late twenties.

"I can't remember what Homer looked like," the widow said. "But he could yodel like nobody's business. Yodelling had just come in." She thought of Lloyd and how he said he and Arby, another brother, had been lucky to get out of California alive after they'd gone there to bring Homer's body back. Homer had been found dead in a fleabag hotel with Lloyd's phone number in his shirt pocket. "They'd as soon knock you in the head in them places as to look at you," Lloyd said afterwards.

"He was a street wino," the widow said to the girl. "But he was a beautiful yodeler. And he could play the guitar too."

"I think my dad used to whistle," the girl said. "I think I remember him whistling." She gazed toward the grove of trees, then across the street to the elementary school building. No one was coming in or going out of the building. It occurred to the widow that she had been to the cemetery hundreds of times and had never once seen any children coming or going from the school. But she knew they did, as surely as she knew that the people buried under the ground had once walked the earth, eaten meals, and answered to their names. She knew this as surely as she knew Homer Medly had been a beautiful yodeler.

"If I died tomorrow, I wonder what my little girls would remember," the girl said suddenly. The widow didn't know what to say to this so she didn't say anything. After a moment the girl said, "I'd like to start bringing my girls with me out here, but I hate to see kids run over the graves."

"I know what you mean," the widow said. But then she thought of her own father. Something he had said when he'd refused to be buried in the big county cemetery back home in Arkansas. "I want to be close enough to home that my grandkids can trample on my grave if they want to." But as it turned out, everyone had moved away, and it hadn't mattered where he was buried.

"I always try to walk at the foot of the graves," the girl said. "But sometimes I forget." She put her hands into the hip pockets of her jeans and looked toward the mausoleum. "Those ones that are ashes, they don't have to worry," she said. She took her hands out of her pockets and sat down again on the grass next to the grave. "Nobody walks over them," she said. "I guess they just sit forever in those little cups."

The widow thought of Homer's remains being contained in a little cup. She was glad she'd never have to see it. Then she remembered that Lloyd had said he and his brother had wanted to bring Homer's body back, but there was too much red tape. And then there was the expense. So they'd had him cremated and, between them, they'd taken turns on the plane holding the box with his ashes in it until they got home. Remembering this made the widow want to say a few words about Homer. She'd met Homer in her girlhood at nearly the same time she'd met her husband. For a moment, the thought came to her that Homer could have been her husband. But just as quickly she dismissed the thought. What had happened to Homer had made a deep, unsettling impression on her. She and Lloyd had talked about it once when they'd spoken in the supermarket. Lloyd had shaken his head and said, "Homer could of been something. He just fell in with the wrong company." And then he hadn't said anything else.

The girl brushed at something on the headstone. "My father was killed in an accident," she said. "We'd all been in swimming and then we kids went to the cabin to nap. My mother woke us up, crying. 'Your daddy's drowned,' she said. This drunk guy tried to swim the river and when my father tried to save him, the man pulled him down. 'Your daddy's drowned,' she kept saying. But you don't understand things when you're a kid," the girl said. "And you don't understand things later either."

The widow was struck by this. She touched her teeth against

her bottom lip, then ran her tongue over the lip. She didn't know what to say, so she said: "There's Homer that lived through the Second World War and then died in California a pure alcoholic." The widow shook her head. She didn't understand any of it.

The girl stretched out on the ground once more and made herself comfortable. She looked up at the widow and nodded once. The widow felt the girl slipping away into a reverie, into some place she couldn't follow, and she wanted to say something to hold her back. But all she could think of was Homer Medly. She couldn't feature why she couldn't get Homer off her mind. She wanted to tell the girl everything that was important to know about Homer Medly. How he had fallen into bad company in the person of Lester Yates, a boy who had molested a young girl and been sent to the penitentiary. How Beulah Looney had gone to the horse races in Santa Rosa, California, in 1935, and brought back word that Homer was married, and to a fine looking woman! But the woman didn't live very long with Homer. He got drunk and hammered out the headlights of their car, then threatened to bite off her nose.

But the widow didn't tell the girl any of this. She couldn't. Besides, the girl looked to be half-asleep. The widow looked down at the girl and it seemed the most natural thing in the world for the girl to be lying there alongside her father's grave. Then the girl raised up on one elbow.

"I came out here the day of my divorce," the girl said. "And then I kept coming out here. One time I lay down and fell asleep," she said. "The caretaker came over and asked me was I alright. Sure, I said. I'm alright." The girl laughed softly and tossed her black hair over her shoulder. "Fact is, I don't know if I was alright. I been coming here trying to figure things out. If my dad was alive I'd ask him what was going to become of me and my girls. There's another man ready to step in and take up where my husband left off. But even if a man runs out on you it's no comfort just to pick up with the next one that comes around.

I got to do better," the girl said. "I got to think of my girls, but I got to think of me too."

The widow felt she'd listened in on something important, and she wished she knew what to say to the girl for comfort. She and her husband hadn't been able to have children and, like so much of her life, she'd reconciled herself to it and never looked back. But now she could imagine having a daughter to talk with and to advise. Someone she could help in a difficult time. She felt she'd missed something precious and that she had nothing to offer the girl except to stand there and listen. Since her husband's death nearly a year ago it seemed that she seldom did more than exchange a few words with people. And here she was telling a stranger about Homer and listening to the girl tell her things back. Her memory of Homer seemed to insist on being told, and though the widow didn't understand why this should be, she felt she'd had a part in it. She didn't want this meeting to end until she'd said what she had to say.

The shadows from the stand of trees had darkened the portion of the cemetery that lay in front of the school building. The girl tilted her head toward the place her father was lying, and the widow thought she might be praying – or about to pray.

"Well, I've got peonies to put out," the widow said, and she moved back a few steps. But the girl did not acknowledge her leaving. The widow waited a minute, then turned and headed back across the graves. The ground felt softer than it had when she'd approached the girl, and she couldn't help thinking that each time she put her foot down she had stepped on someone.

She felt relieved when she reached her husband's grave. She stood on the grave as if there at least she had a right to do as she pleased. The grave was like a green island in the midst of other green islands. Then she heard a car start up. She turned to look for the girl, but the girl was no longer there. The girl was gone. Just then the widow saw a little red car head out of the cemetery.

The widow took hold of her flowers and began to fit them into a vase next to the flowers she guessed must be from Lloyd. Once, a few weeks earlier, Lloyd had stopped at her house on the way to the cemetery and she'd given him some flowers to take to Homer and some for her husband. "They were roarers, those two," Lloyd had said as she'd made up the two bouquets. She thought of her husband again. He'd been a drinker like Homer and, except for having married her, he might have fallen in with bad company and ended the way Homer had.

She took her watering can and walked toward the spigot that stood near the mausoleum. She bent down and ran water into the can as she rested her eyes on the mausoleum. Bad company, she thought. And it occurred to her that her husband had been *her* bad company for all those years. And when he hadn't been bad company, he'd been no company at all to her. She listened to the water run into the metal can and wondered what had saved her from being pulled down by the likes of such a man, even as Lester Yates had pulled Homer Medly down.

She let herself recall the time her husband had flown into a rage after a drinking bout and accused her of sleeping around, even though every night of their married life she'd slept nowhere but in the same bed with him. He'd taken her set of china cups out onto the sidewalk and smashed them with the whole neighborhood looking on. From then on they'd passed their evenings in silence. She would knit and he would look after the fire and smoke cigarettes. It was a life to be reckoned with, and God knows she'd done the best she could. But the memory of those long, silent evenings struck at her heart now, and she wished she could go back to that time and speak to her husband. She knew there were old couples who lived differently, couples who took walks together or played checkers or cards together in the evenings. And then it came to her that she had been bad company to him, had even denied him her company, going and coming from the house with barely a nod in his direction, putting his meals on the table out of duty alone, keeping house like a jailer. The idea startled and pained her, especially when she remembered how his illness had come on him until, in the last months, he was docile and then finally helpless near the end. What had she given him? What had she done for him? She could answer only that she had been there – like an implement, a shovel or a hoe, maybe. A lifetime of robbery! she thought. Then she understood that it was herself she had robbed as much as her husband. And there was no way now to get it back.

The water was running over the sides of the can, and she turned off the spigot. She picked up the watering can and stood next to the mausoleum and stared at it as if someone had suddenly thrown an obstacle in her pathway. She couldn't feature why anyone would want to be put into such a place when they died. The front was faced with rough stones and one wall was mostly glass so that visitors could peer inside. The widow had tried the door to this place once, but it was locked. She supposed the relatives had keys, or else they were let in by the caretaker. Homer was situated along the wall on the outside of the mausoleum. Thinking of Homer made her glad her husband hadn't ended up on the wall of the mausoleum as a pile of ashes. There was that to be thankful for.

When she reached his grave she poured water into the vase and then stared at the bronze name plate where enough space had been left for her own name and dates.

She remembered the day she and her husband had quarreled about where to buy their burial plots. Her husband had said he wasn't about to be buried any place that was likely to cave into the ocean. He said this because there were two cemeteries in their town – this one just off the main highway near the elementary school, and the other which was located at the edge of a cliff overlooking the ocean. He did not want to be near the ocean. He said this several times. Then he had gone down and purchased two plots side by side across from the school and close to the mausoleum. She hadn't said much. Then he had shown her the papers with the location of the graves marked with little Xs on a map of the cemetery. The more she thought about it though, the more she set her mind on buying her own plot in the cemetery overlooking the ocean. Then one day she arranged to go there, and she paid for a gravesite that very day.

She hadn't meant to tell her husband about her purchase, but one night they'd quarreled bitterly, and she'd flung the news at him. She had *two* gravesites she said – one with him and one away from him; and she would do as she pleased when the time came. "Take your old bones and throw them in the ocean for all I care," he told her.

They'd left it like that. Right up until he died, her husband hadn't known where his wife was going to be buried. But what a thing to have done to him! To have denied him even that small comfort. She realized now that if anyone had told her about a woman who had done such a thing to a dying husband she would have been shocked and ashamed for her. But this was the story of herself she was considering, and she was the one who'd sent her life's company lonely to the grave. This thought was so painful to her she felt her body go rigid – as if some force had struck her from the outside, and she had to brace herself to bear it.

She'd taken comfort in the idea of the second grave, even when she couldn't make up her mind where she would finally lay. She had prolonged her decision and she saw this clearly now for what it was, a way to deny this man with whom she had spent her life. Even when she came to the cemetery where her husband lay, she would still be thinking, as she was now, about the cemetery near the ocean – how when she went there she could gaze out at the little fishing boats on the water or listen to the gulls as they wheeled over the bluff. An oil tanker or a freighter might appear and slide serenely across the horizon. She loved how slowly the ships passed, and how she could follow them with her eyes until they were lost in the distance.

She gave the watering can a shake. There was water left in it, and she raised the can to her lips and drank deeply and thought again of the ocean. What she loved about that view was the thought too that those who walked in a cemetery, any cemetery, ought to be able to forget the dead for a moment and gaze out at something larger than themselves. Something mysterious. The ocean tantalized her even as she felt a kind of foreboding when she looked on it with her own death in mind. She could imagine children galloping over the graves, then coming to a stop at the sharp edge of the cliff to stare down at the waves far below. Her visits to the cemetery near the ocean gave her pleasure even after her grave there was no longer a secret. When her husband asked, "Have you been out there?" she knew what he meant. "I have," she said. And that was the extent of it. Then he had died, and some of the pleasure in her visits to the other grave seemed to have gone with him.

As the widow's life alone settled into its own routine, weeks might go by until, with a start, she would realize she hadn't been to either cemetery. The fact of her two graves became a mystery to her. She thought she understood the torment of those who committed adulterous acts and then returned home – unfaithful and unrepentant. Yet she did nothing to change the situation.

The shadows of the evergreens had reached where she was standing. She saw that the school building across the street was entirely in shadow now. She gathered up the containers she'd used to carry flowers to the grave and picked up her garden shears. On her way to the car she turned and looked at the flowers on her husband's grave. They seemed to accuse her of something paltry, of some falsehood. She had decorated his grave, but there was no comfort in it for her. No comfort, she thought, and she knew she had simply been dutiful toward her husband in death as she had been in life. The thought quickened her step away from there. She reached her car and got in. Her breath was coming hard and unevenly and for a moment she could not think where it was she was supposed to go next.

A MONTH HAD PASSED since her visit to the cemetery. Daisies and carnations were in bloom, but the widow hadn't been back to her husband's grave. It was early on a Sunday when she decided to go again. She expected the cemetery to be empty at that time of the morning, but no sooner had she arrived than a little red car drove into the narrow roadway through the cemetery and parked near the mausoleum. Then the driver got out.

The widow was not surprised to see that it was the young woman she'd met on her last visit. The widow felt glad when the girl raised her hand in greeting as she passed on her way to her father's grave.

The girl stood by the grave with her head down, thinking. She had on a short red coat and a dress this time, like she might be on her way to church. The widow approved of this – that the girl was dressed up and that she might go on to church. This caused another kind of respect to come into the visit. But what the widow felt most of all, was that this was a wonderful coincidence. She had met the girl twice now in the cemetery and she wondered at this. She thought it must mean something, but she couldn't think what.

The widow took the dead flowers from the vases and emptied the acrid water. There was a stench as if the water itself had a body that could be corrupted. She remembered a time in her girlhood when she and Homer and her husband had been driving to a country dance in the next county. The car radiator had boiled over and they'd walked to a farm and asked for water. The farmer had given them some in a big glass jug. "It's fine for your car, but I wouldn't drink it," the man said. But the day was hot and after they'd filled the radiator each of them lifted the jug and took a drink. The water tasted like something had died in it. "Jesus save me from water like that!" Homer had said. "They invented whiskey to cover up water like that." Her husband agreed that the water tasted bad, but he took another drink anyway. "I was thirsty," he said.

The widow straightened and glanced again toward the girl. She seemed deep in thought as she stood beside the grave. The widow saw that once again she had brought no flowers with her.

"Would you like some flowers for your grave?" the widow called to her. The girl looked startled, as if the idea had never occurred to her. She waited a moment. Then she smiled and nodded. The widow busied herself choosing flowers from her own bunch to make a modest bouquet. Then she stepped carefully over the graves toward the girl. The girl took the flowers and pressed them to her face to smell them, as if these were the first flowers she'd held in a long time.

"I love carnations," she said. Then, before the widow could stop her, the girl began to dig a hole with her fingers at the top of her father's headstone.

"Wait! Just a minute," the widow said. "I'll find something." She walked to her car and found a jar in the trunk. She returned with this and the girl walked with her toward the mausoleum to draw water to fill the container. The water spigot was near the corner of the mausoleum where Homer's ashes lay, and the widow remembered having told the girl about his death.

"There's Homer," the widow said, and pointed to the wall of the mausoleum. There were four name plates to each marble block and near each name a small fluted vase was attached to the stone. Most of the vases had faded plastic flowers in them, but Homer's vase was empty. The girl opened and closed her black eyes, then lifted her flowers and poured a little of the fresh water into the container fastened to Homer's stone. Then she took two carnations and fitted them into the vase. It was the right thing to do and the widow felt as if she'd done it herself.

As they walked back toward the graves the widow had the impulse to tell the girl about her gravesite near the ocean. But before she could say anything, the girl said, "I've got what I came for. I been coming here and asking what it is I'm supposed to do with my life. Well, I'm not for sale. That's what he let me know. I'm free now and I'm going to stay free," the girl said. The widow heard the word "free" as if from a great distance. *Free* she thought, but the word was meaningless to her. It came to her that in all her visits to her husband's grave she'd gotten nothing she needed. She'd just as well go and stand in her own backyard for all she got there. But she didn't let on to the girl she was feeling any of this, and when they set the container of carnations on the grave she said only, "That's better, isn't it."

"Yes," the girl said. "Yes, it is." She seemed then to want to be alone, so the widow made her way back to her husband's grave. But after a few minutes she saw that instead of staying around to enjoy the flowers, the girl was leaving. She waved toward the widow and the widow thought, *I'll never see her again.* Before she could bring herself to lift her hand to wave goodbye, the girl got into her car. Then the motor started, and she watched the car drive out of the cemetery.

A WEEK LATER the widow drove to the cemetery again. She looked around as she got out of the car, half expecting to see the little red car drive up and the girl get out. But she knew this wouldn't happen. At her husband's grave she cleared away the dead flowers from her last visit.

The widow had brought no flowers and didn't quite know what to do with herself. She looked past the mausoleum and saw that a new field was being cleared to make room for additional graves at the far end of the cemetery. The sight brought a feeling of such desolation that she shuddered. She felt more alone than she had ever felt in her life. For the first time she realized she would continue on this way, alone to the end. Her whole body ached with the dull hopelessness of the feeling. She felt that if she had to speak she would have no voice. She was glad that the girl wasn't there, that she would not have to speak to anyone in this place of regret and loneliness. Suddenly the caretaker came out of a shed in the trees, turned on a sprinkler and disappeared back into the shed. Then, once again, there was no one.

She waited a minute, and then lowered herself onto the grave. The water from the sprinkler whirled and looped over the graves, but it did not reach as far as her husband's grave. She looked around her, but there was no one to be seen. She leaned back on the grave and stretched out her legs. She put her head on the ground and closed her eyes. The sun was warm on her face and arms and she began to feel drowsy.

As she lay there she thought she heard children running and laughing somewhere in the cemetery. But she couldn't separate this sound from the sound of the water, and she did not open her eyes to see if there really were children. The sprinkler made a *whit-whit* noise like a scythe going through a field of tall grass.

"I'm going to rest here a moment," she said out loud without opening her eyes. Then she said, "I've decided. You bought a place for me here, and that's what you wanted. And that's what I want too."

She opened her eyes then and with an awful certainty she knew that her husband had heard nothing of what she had said. And not in all of time would he hear her. She'd cut herself off from him as someone too good, someone too proud to do anything but injury to the likes of him. And this was her reward, that it would not matter to anyone on the face of the earth that she had ever lived. This, she thought, was eternity – to be left so utterly alone and to know that even her choice to be buried next to him would never reach her husband. Was she any better than the meanest wino who died in some fleabag hotel and was eventually reduced to ashes? No, she understood, no better. She had been no better than her husband all those years, and if she had saved him from a death like Homer's, it was only to die disowned at her own hearth. The enormity of this settled on her as she struggled to raise herself up.

A light mist from the sprinkler touched her face, and when she looked around her, she saw a vastness like that of the ocean. Headstones marked off the grass as far as she could see. She saw plainly a silent and fixed company set out there, a company she had not chosen.

She looked and saw the caretaker in the doorway of the shed. He drew on his cigarette as he stood watching her. She raised her hand and then brought it down to let him know she had seen him. He inclined his head and went on smoking.

MAVIS GALLANT

Irina

ONE OF IRINA'S GRANDSONS, nicknamed Riri, was sent to her at Christmas. His mother was going into hospital, but nobody told him that. The real cause of his visit was that since Irina had become a widow her children worried about her being alone. The children, as Irina would call them forever, were married and in their thirties and forties. They did not think they were like other people, because their father had been a powerful old man. He was a Swiss writer, Richard Notte. They carried his reputation and the memory of his puritan equity like an immense jar filled with water of which they had been told not to spill a drop. They loved their mother, but they had never needed to think about her until now. They had never fretted about which way her shadow might fall, and whether to stay in the shade or get out by being eccentric and bold. There were two sons and three daughters, with fourteen children among them. Only Riri was an only child. The girls had married an industrial designer, a Lutheran minister (perhaps an insolent move, after all, for the daughter of a militant atheist), and an art historian in Paris. One boy had become a banker and the other a lecturer on Germanic musical tradition. These were the crushed sons and loyal daughters to whom Irina had been faithful, whose pictures had travelled with her and lived beside her bed.

Few of Notte's obituaries had even mentioned a family. Some of his literary acquaintances were surprised to learn there had been any children at all, though everyone paid homage to the soft, quiet wife to whom he had dedicated his books, the subject of his first rapturous poems. These poems, conventional verse for the most part, seldom translated out of German except by unpoetical research scholars, were thought to be the work of his youth. Actually, Notte was forty when he finally married, and Irina barely nineteen. The obituaries called Notte the last of a breed, the end of a Tolstoyan line of moral lightning rods – an extinction which was probably hard on those writers who came after him, and still harder on his children. However, even to his family the old man had appeared to be the very archetype of a respected European novelist – prophet, dissuader, despairingly opposed to evil, crack-voiced after having made so many pronouncements. Otherwise, he was not all that typical as a Swiss or as a Western, liberal, Protestant European, for he neither saved, nor invested, nor hid, nor disguised his material returns.

"What good is money, except to give away?" he often said. He had a wife, five children, and an old secretary who had turned into a dependent. It was true that he claimed next to nothing for himself. He rented shabby, ramshackle houses impossible to heat or even to clean. Owning was against his convictions, and he did not want to be tied to a gate called home. His room was furnished with a cot, a lamp, a desk, two chairs, a map of the world, a small bookshelf – no more, not even carpets or curtains. Like his family, he wore thick sweaters indoors as out, and crouched over inadequate electric fires. He seldom ate meat – though he did not deprive his children – and drank water with his meals. He had married once – once and for all. He could on occasion enjoy wine and praise and restaurants and good-looking women, but these festive outbreaks were on the rim of his real life, as remote from his children – as strange and as distorted to them – as some other country's colonial wars. He grew old early, as if he expected old age to suit him. By sixty, his eyes were sunk in pockets of lizard skin. His hair became bleached and lustrous, like the scrap of wedding dress Irina kept in a jeweller's box. He was photographed wearing a dark suit and a woman's plaid shawl – he was always cold by then, even in summer – and with a rakish felt hat shading half his face. His wife still let a few photographers in, at the end – but not many. Her murmured "He is working" had for decades been a double lock. He was as strong as Rasputin, his enemies said; he went on writing and talking and travelling until he positively could not focus his eyes or be helped aboard a train. Nearly to the last, he and Irina swung off on their seasonal cycle of journeys to Venice, to Rome, to cities where their married children lived, to Liége and Oxford for awards and honors. His place in a hotel dining room was recognizable from the door because of the pills, drops, and powders lined up to the width of a dinner plate. Notte's hypochondria had been known and gently caricatured for years. His sons, between them, had now bought up most of the original drawings: Notte, in infant's clothing, downing his medicine like a man (he had missed the Nobel); Notte quarrelling with Aragon and throwing up Surrealism; a grim female figure called "Existentialism" taking his pulse; Notte catching Asian flu on a cultural trip to Peking. During the final months of his life his children noticed that their mother had begun acquiring medicines of her own, as if hoping by means of mirror-magic to draw his ailments into herself.

If illness became him, it was only because he was fond of ritual, the children thought – even the hideous ceremonial of pain. But Irina had not been intended for sickness and suffering; she was meant to be burned dry and consumed by the ritual of him. The children believed that the end of his life would surely be the death of their mother. They did not really expect Irina to turn her face to the wall and die, but an exclusive, even a selfish, alliance with Notte had seemed her reason for being. As their father grew old, then truly old, then old in mind, and querulous, and unjust, they observed the patient tenderness with which she heeded his sulks and caprices, his almost insane commands. They supposed this ardent submission of hers had to do with love, but it was not a sort of love they had ever experienced or tried to provoke. One of his sons saw Notte crying because Irina had buttered toast for him when he wanted it dry. She stroked the old man's silky hair, smiling. The son hated this. Irina was diminishing a strong, proud man, making a senile child of him, just as Notte was enslaving and debasing her. At the same time the son felt a secret between the two, a mystery. He wondered then, but at no other time, if the secret might not be Irina's invention and property.

Notte left a careful will for such an unworldly person. His wife was to be secure in her lifetime. Upon her death the residue of income from his work would be shared among the sons and daughters. There were no gifts or bequests. The will was accompanied by a testament which the children had photocopied for the beauty of the handwriting and the charm of the text. Irina, it began, belonged to a generation of women shielded from decisions, allowed to grow in the sun and shade of male protection. This flower, his flower, he wrote, was to be cherished now as if she were her children's child.

"In plain words," said Irina, at the first reading, in a Zurich lawyer's office, "I am the heir." She was wearing dark glasses because her eyes were tired, and a tight hat. She looked tense and foreign.

Well, yes, that was it, although Notte had put it more gracefully. His favorite daughter was his literary executor, entrusted with the unfinished manuscripts and the journals he had kept for sixty-five years. But it soon became evident that Irina had no intention of giving these up. The children adored their mother, but even without love as a factor would not have made a case of it; Notte's lawyer had already told them about disputes ending in mazelike litigation, families sundered, contents of a desk sequestered, diaries rotting in bank vaults while the inheritors thrashed it out. Besides, editing Notte's papers would keep Irina busy and an occupation was essential now. In loving and unloving families alike, the same problem arises after a death: What to do about the widow?

Irina settled some of it by purchasing an apartment in a small Alpine town. She chose a tall, glassy, urban-looking building of the kind that made conservationist groups send round-robin letters, accompanied by incriminating photographs, to newspapers in Lausanne. The apartment had a hall, an up-to-date kitchen, a bedroom for Irina, a spare room with a narrow bed in it, one bathroom, and a living room containing a couch. There was a glassed-in cube of a balcony where in a pinch an extra cot might have fitted, but Irina used the space for a table and chairs. She ordered red lampshades and thick curtains and the pale furniture that is usually sold to young couples. She seemed to come into her own in that tight, neutral flat, the children thought. They read some of the interviews she gave, and approved: she said, in English and Italian, in German and French, that she would not be a literary widow, detested by critics, resented by Notte's readers. Her firm diffidence made the children smile, and they were proud to read about her dignified beauty. But as for her intelligence – well, they supposed that the interviewers had confused fluency with wit. Irina's views and her way of expressing them were all camouflage, simply part of a ladylike undereducation, long on languages and bearing, short on history and arithmetic. Her origins were Russian and Swiss and probably pious; the children had not been drawn to that side of the family. Their father's legendary peasant childhood, his isolated valley-village had filled their imaginations and their collective past. There was a sudden April lightness in her letters now that relieved and yet troubled them. They knew it was a sham happiness, Nature's way of protecting the survivor from immediate grief. The crisis would come later, when her most secret instincts had built a seawall. They took turns invading her at Easter and in the summer, one couple at a time, bringing a child apiece – there was no room for more. Winter was a problem, however, for the skiing was not good just there, and none of them liked to break up their families at Christmastime. Not only was Irina's apartment lacking in beds but there was absolutely no space for a tree. Finally, she offered to visit them, in regular order. That was how they settled it. She went to Bern, to Munich, to Zurich, and then came the inevitable Christmas when it was not that no one wanted her but just that they were all doing different things.

She had written in November of that year that a friend, whom she described, with some quaintness, as "a person," had come for a long stay. They liked that. A visit meant winter company, lamps on at four, China tea, conversation, the peppery smell of carnations (her favorite flower) in a warm room. For a week or two of the visit her letters were blithe, but presently they noticed that "the person" seemed to be having a depressing effect on their mother. She wrote that she had been working on Notte's journals for three years now. Who would want to read them except old men and women? His moral and political patterns were fossils of liberalism. He had seen the cracks in the Weimar Republic. He had understood from the beginning what Hitler meant. If at first he had been wrong about Mussolini, he had changed his mind even before Croce changed his, and had been safely back on the side of democracy in time to denounce Pirandello. He had given all he could, short of his life, to the Spanish Republicans. His measure of Stalin had been so wise and unshakably just that he had never been put on the Communist index – something rare for a Western Socialist. No one could say, ever, that Notte had hedged or retreated or kept silent when a voice was needed. Well, said Irina, what of it? He had written, pledged, warned, signed, declared. And what had he changed, diverted, or stopped? She suddenly sent the same letter to all five children: "This Christmas I don't want to go anywhere. I intend to stay here, in my own home."

They knew this was the crisis and that they must not leave her to face it alone, but that was the very winter when all their plans ran down, when one daughter was going into hospital, another moving to a different city, the third probably divorcing. The elder son was committed to a Christmas with his wife's parents, the younger lecturing in South Africa – a country where Irina, as Notte's constant reflection, would certainly not wish to set foot. They wrote and called and cabled one another: What shall we do? Can you? Will you? I can't.

Irina had no favorites among her children, except possibly one son who had been ill with rheumatic fever as a child and required long nursing. To him she now confided that she longed for her own childhood sometimes, in order to avoid having to judge herself. She was homesick for a time when nothing had crystallized and mistakes were allowed. Now, in old age, she had no excuse for errors. Every thought had a long meaning; every motive had angles and corners, and could be measured. And yet whatever she saw and thought and attempted was still fluid and vague. The shape of a table against afternoon light still held a mystery, awaited a final explanation. You looked for clarity, she wrote, and the answer you had was paleness, the flat white cast that a snowy sky throws across a room

Part of this son knew about death and dying, but the rest of him was a banker and thoroughly active. He believed that, given an ideal situation, one should be able to walk through a table, which would save time and roundabout decisions. However, like all of Notte's children he had been raised with every awareness of solid matter too. His mother's youthful, yearning, and probably religious letter made him feel bland and old. He told his wife what he thought it contained, and she told a sister-in-law what she thought he had said. Irina was tired. Her eyesight was poor, perhaps as a result of prolonged work on those diaries. Irina did not need adult company, which might lead to morbid conversation; what she craved now was a symbol of innocent, continuing life. An animal might do it. Better still, a child.

RIRI DID NOT KNOW that his mother would be in hospital the minute his back was turned. Balanced against a tame Christmas with a grandmother was a midterm holiday, later, of high-altitude skiing with his father. There was also some further blackmail involving his holiday homework, and then the vague state of behavior called "being reasonable" – that was all anyone asked. They celebrated a token Christmas on the twenty-third, and the next day he packed his presents (a watch and a tape recorder) and was put on a plane at Orly West. He flew from Paris to Geneva, where he spent the real Christmas Eve in a strange, bare apartment into which an aunt and a large family of cousins had just moved. In the morning he was wakened when it was dark and taken to a six-o'clock train. He said goodbye to his aunt at the station, and added, "If you ask the conductor or anyone to look after me, I'll – " Whatever threat was in his mind he seemed ready to carry it out. He wore an R.A.F. badge on his jacket and carried a Waffen-S.S. emblem in his pocket. He knew better than to keep it in sight. At home they had already taken one away but he had acquired another at school. He had Astérix comic books for reading, chocolate-covered hazelnuts for support, and his personal belongings in a fairly large knapsack. He made a second train on his own and got down at the right station.

He had been told that he knew this place, but his memory, if it was a memory, had to do with fields and a picnic. No one met him. He shared a taxi through soft snow with two women, and paid his share – actually more than his share, which annoyed the women; they could not give less than a child in the way of a tip. The taxi let him off at a dark, shiny tower on stilts with granite steps. In the lobby a marble panel, looking like the list of names of war dead in his school, gave him his grandmother on the eighth floor. The lift, like the façade of the building, was made of dark mirrors into which he gazed seriously. A dense, thoughtful person looked back. He took off his glasses and the blurred face became even more remarkable. His grandmother had both a bell and a knocker at her door. He tried both. For quite a long time nothing happened. He knocked and rang again. It was not nervousness that he felt but a new sensation that had to do with a shut, foreign door.

His grandmother opened the door a crack. She had short white hair and a pale face and blue eyes. She held a dressing gown gripped at the collar. She flung the door back and cried, "Darling Richard, I thought you were arriving much later. Oh," she said, "I must look dreadful to you. Imagine finding me like this, in my dressing gown!" She tipped her head away and talked between her fingers, as he had been told never to do, because only liars cover their mouths. He saw a dark hall and a bright kitchen that was in some disorder, and a large dark, curtained room opposite the kitchen. This room smelled stuffy, of old cigarettes and of adults. But then his grandmother pushed the draperies apart and wound up the slatted shutters, and what had been dark, moundlike objects turned into a couch and a bamboo screen and a round table and a number of chairs. On a bookshelf stood a painting of three tulips that must have fallen out of their vase. Behind them was a sky that was all black except for a rainbow. He unpacked a portion of the things in his knapsack – wrapped presents for his grandmother, his new tape recorder, two school textbooks, a notebook, a Bic pen. The start of this Christmas lay hours behind him and his breakfast had died long ago.

"Are you hungry?" said his grandmother. He heard a telephone ringing as she brought him a cup of hot milk with a little coffee in it and two fresh croissants on a plate. She was obviously someone who never rushed to answer any bell. "My friend, who is an early riser, even on Christmas Day, went out and got these croissants. Very bravely, I thought." He ate his new breakfast, dipping the croissants in the milk, and heard his grandmother saying, "Well, I must have misunderstood. But he managed.... He didn't bring his skis. Why not?...I see." By the time she came back he had a book open. She watched him for a second and said, "Do you read at meals at home?"

"Sometimes."

"That's not the way I brought up your mother."

He put his nose nearer the page without replying. He read aloud from the page in a soft schoolroom plain-chant: "Go, went, gone. Stand, stood, stood. Take, took, taken."

"Richard," said his grandmother. When he did not look up at once, she said, "I know what they call you at home, but what are you called in school?"

"Riri."

"I have three Richard grandsons," she said, "and not one is called Richard exactly."

"I have an Uncle Richard," he said.

"Yes, well, he happens to be a son of mine. I never allowed nicknames. Have you finished your breakfast?"

"Yes."

"Yes who? Yes what? What is your best language, by the way?"

"I am French," he said, with a sharp, sudden, hard hostility, the first tense bud of it, that made her murmur, "So soon?" She was about to tell him that he was not French – at least, not really – when an old man came into the room. He was thin and walked with a cane.

"Alec, this is my grandson," she said. "Riri, say how do you do to Mr. Aiken, who was kind enough to go out in this morning's snow to buy croissants for us all."

"I knew he would be here early," said the old man, in a stiff French that sounded extremely comical to the boy. "Irina has an odd ear for times and trains." He sat down next to Riri and clasped his hands on his cane; his hands at once began to tremble violently. "What does that interesting-looking book tell you?" he asked.

"'The swallow flew away,'" answered Irina, reading over the child's head. "'The swallow flew away with my hopes.'"

"Good God, let me look at that!" said the old man in his funny French. Sure enough, those were the words, and there was a swallow of a very strange blue, or at least a sapphire-and-turquoise creature with a swallow's tail. Riri's grandmother took her spectacles out of her dressing-gown pocket and brought the book up close and said in a loud, solemn way, "'The swallows will have flown away.'" Then she picked up the tape recorder, which was the size of a glasses case, and after snapping the wrong button on and off, causing agonizing confusion and wastage, she said with her mouth against it, "'When shall the swallows have flown away?'"

"No," said Riri, reaching, snatching almost. As if she had always given in to men, even to male children, she put the book down and the recorder too, saying, "Mr. Aiken can help with your English. He has the best possible accent. When he says 'the girl' you will think he is saying 'de Gaulle.'"

"Irina has an odd ear for English," said the old man calmly. He got up slowly and went to the kitchen, and she did too, and Riri could hear them whispering and laughing at something. Mr. Aiken came back alone carrying a small glass of clear liquid. "The morning heart-starter," he said. "Try it." Riri took a sip. It lay in his stomach like a warm stone. "No more effect on you than a gulp of milk," said the old man, marvelling, sitting down close to Riri again. "You could probably do with pints of this stuff. I can tell by looking at you you'll be a drinking man." His hands on the walking stick began to tremble anew. "I'm not the man I was," he said. "Not by any means." Because he did not speak English with a French or any foreign accent, Riri could not really understand him. He went on, "Fell down the staircase at the Trouville casino. Trouville, or that other place. Shock gave me amnesia. Hole in the stair carpet – must have been. I went there for years," he said. "Never saw a damned hole in anything. Now my hands shake."

"When you lift your glass to drink they don't shake," called Riri's grandmother from the kitchen. She repeated this in French, for good measure.

"She's got an ear like a radar unit," said Mr. Aiken.

Riri took up his tape recorder. In a measured chant, as if demonstrating to his grandmother how these things should be done, he said, "'The swallows would not fly away if the season is fine.'"

"Do you know what any of it means?" said Mr. Aiken.

"He doesn't need to know what it means," Riri's grandmother answered for him. "He just needs to know it by heart."

THEY WERE GLASSED IN on the balcony. The only sound they could hear was of their own voices. The sun on them was so hot that Riri wanted to take off his sweater. Looking down, he saw a chalet crushed in the shadows of two white blocks, not so tall as their own. A large, spared spruce tree suddenly seemed to retract its branches and allow a great weight of snow to slip off. Cars went by, dogs barked, children called – all in total silence. His grandmother talked English to the old man. Riri, when he was not actually eating, read *Astérix in Brittany* without attracting her disapproval.

"If people can be given numbers, like marks in school," she said, "then children are zero." She was enveloped in a fur cloak, out of which her hands and arms emerged as if the fur had dissolved in certain places. She was pink with wine and sun. The old man's blue eyes were paler than hers. "Zero." She held up thumb and forefinger in an O. "I was there with my five darling zeros while he... You are probably wondering if I was *ever* happy. At the beginning, in the first days, when I thought he would give me interesting books to read, books that would change all my life. Riri," she said, shading her eyes, "the cake and ice cream were, I am afraid, the end of things for the moment. Could I ask you to clear the table for me?"

"I don't at home." Nevertheless he made a wobbly pile of dishes and took them away and did not come back. They heard him, indoors, starting all over: "'Go, went, gone.'"

"I have only half a memory for dates," she said. "I forget my children's birthdays until the last minute and have to send them telegrams. But I know *that* day...."

"The twenty-sixth of May," he said. "What I forget is the year."

"I know that I felt young."

"You were. You *are* young," he said.

"Except that I was forty if a day." She glanced at the hands and wrists emerging from her cloak as if pleased at their whiteness. "The river was so sluggish, I remember. And the willows trailed in the river."

"Actually, there was a swift current after the spring rains."

"But no wind. The clouds were heavy."

"It was late in the afternoon," he said. "We sat on the grass."

"On a raincoat. You had thought in the morning those clouds meant rain."

"A young man drowned," he said. "Fell out of a boat. Funny, he didn't try to swim. So people kept saying."

"We saw three firemen in gleaming metal helmets. They fished for him so languidly – the whole day was like that. They had a grappling hook. None of them knew what to do with it. They kept pulling it up and taking the rope from each other."

"They might have been after water lilies, from the look of them."

"One of them bailed out the boat with a blue saucepan. I remember that. They'd got that saucepan from the restaurant."

"Where we had lunch," he said. "Trout, and a coffee cream pudding. You left yours."

"It was soggy cake. But the trout was perfection. So was the wine. The bridge over the river filled up slowly with holiday people. The three firemen rowed to shore."

"Yes, and one of them went off on a shaky bicycle and came back with a coil of frayed rope on his shoulders."

"The railway station was just behind us. All those people on the bridge were waiting for a train. When the firemen's boat slipped off down the river, they moved without speaking from one side of the bridge to the other, just to watch the boat. The silence of it."

"Like the silence here."

"This is a planned silence," she said.

Riri played back his own voice. A tinny, squeaky Riri said, "'Go, went, gone. Eat, ate, eaten. See, saw, sen.'"

"'Seen'!" called his grandmother from the balcony. "'Seen,' not 'sen.' His mother made exactly that mistake," she said to the old man. "Oh, stop that," she said. He was crying. "Please, please stop that. How could I have left five children?"

"Three were grown," he gasped, wiping his eyes.

"But they didn't know it. They didn't know they were grown. They still don't know it. And it made six children, counting him."

"The secretary mothered him," he said. "All he needed."

"I know, but you see she wasn't his wife, and he liked saying to strangers 'my wife,' 'my wife this,' 'my wife that.' What is it, Riri? Have you come to finish doing the thing I asked?"

He moved close to the table. His round glasses made him look desperate and stern. He said, "Which room is mine?" Darkness had gathered around him in spite of the sparkling sky and a row of icicles gleaming and melting in the most dazzling possible light. Outrage, a feeling that consideration had been wanting – that was how homesickness had overtaken him. She held his hand (he did not resist – another sign of his misery) and together they explored the apartment. He saw it all – every picture and cupboard and doorway – and in the end it was he who decided that Mr. Aiken must keep the spare room and he, Riri, would be happy on the living room couch.

The old man passed them in the hall; he was obviously about to rest on the very bed he had just been within an inch of losing. He carried a plastic bottle of Evian. "Do you like the bland taste of water?" he said.

Riri looked boldly at his grandmother and said, "Yes," bursting into unexplained and endless-seeming laughter. He seemed to feel a relief at this substitute for impertinence. The old man laughed too, but broke off, coughing.

At half past four, when the windows were as black as the sky in the painting of tulips and began to reflect the lamps in a disturbing sort of way, they drew the curtains and had tea around the table. They pushed Riri's books and belongings to one side and spread a cross-stitched tablecloth. Riri had hot chocolate, a croissant left from breakfast and warmed in the oven, which made it deliciously greasy and soft, a slice of lemon sponge cake, and a banana. This time he helped clear away and even remained in the kitchen, talking, while his grandmother rinsed the cups and plates and stacked them in the machine.

The old man sat on a chair in the hall struggling with snow boots. He was going out alone in the dark to post some letters and to buy a newspaper and to bring back whatever provisions he thought were required for the evening meal.

"Riri, do you want to go with Mr. Aiken? Perhaps you should have a walk."

"At home I don't have to."

His grandmother looked cross; no, she looked worried. She was biting something back. The old man had finished the contention with his boots and now he put on a scarf, a fur-lined coat, a fur hat with earflaps, woollen gloves, and he took a list and a shopping bag and a different walking stick, which looked something like a ski pole. His grandmother stood still, as if dreaming, and then (addressing Riri) decided to wash all her amber necklaces. She fetched a wicker basket from her bedroom. It was lined with orange silk and filled with strings of beads. Riri followed her to the bathroom and sat on the end of the tub. She rolled up her soft sleeves and scrubbed the amber with laundry soap and a stiff brush. She scrubbed and rinsed and then began all over again.

"I am good at things like this," she said. "Now, unless you hate to discuss it, tell me something about your school."

At first he had nothing to say, but then he told her how stupid the younger boys were and what they were allowed to get away with.

"The younger boys would be seven, eight?" Yes, about that. "A hopeless generation?"

He wasn't sure; he knew that his class had been better.

She reached down and fetched a bottle of something from behind the bathtub and they went back to the sitting room together. They put a lamp between them, and Irina began to polish the amber with cotton soaked in turpentine. After a time the amber began to shine. The smell made him homesick, but not unpleasantly. He carefully selected a necklace when she told him he might take one for his mother, and he rubbed it with a soft cloth. She showed him how to make the beads magnetic by rolling them in his palms.

"You can do that even with plastic," he said.

"Can you? How very sad. It is dead matter."

"Amber is too," he said politely.

"What do you want to be later on? A scientist?"

"A ski instructor." He looked all around the room, at the shelves and curtains and at the bamboo folding screen, and said, "If you didn't live here, who would?"

She replied, "If you see anything that pleases you, you may keep it. I want you to choose your own present. If you don't see anything, we'll go out tomorrow and look in the shops. Does that suit you?" He did not reply. She held the necklace he had picked and said, "Your mother will remember seeing this as I bent down to kiss her good night. Do you like old coins? One of my sons was a collector." In the wicker basket was a lacquered box that contained his uncle's coin collection. He took a coin but it meant nothing to him; he let it fall. It clinked, and he said, "We have a dog now." The dog wore a metal tag that rang when the dog drank out of a china bowl. Through a sudden rainy blur of new homesickness he saw that she had something else, another lacquered box, full of old cancelled stamps. She showed him a stamp with Hitler and one with an Italian king. "I've kept funny things," she said. "Like this beautiful Russian box. It belonged to my grandmother, but after I have died I expect it will be thrown out. I gave whatever jewelry I had left to my daughters. We never had furniture, so I became attached to strange little baskets and boxes of useless things. My poor daughters – I had precious little to give. But they won't be able to wear rings any more than I could. We all come into our inherited arthritis, these knotted-up hands. Our true heritage. When I was your age, about, my mother was dying of...I wasn't told. She took a ring from under her pillow and folded my hand on it. She said that I could always sell it if I had to, and no one need know. You see, in those days women had nothing of their own. They were like brown paper parcels tied with string. They were handed like parcels from their fathers to their husbands. To make the parcel look attractive it was decked with curls and piano lessons, and rings and gold coins and banknotes and shares. After appraising all the decoration, the new owner would undo the knots."

"Where is that ring?" he said. The blur of tears was forgotten.

"I tried to sell it when I needed money. The decoration on the brown paper parcel was disposed of by then. Everything thrown, given away. Not by me. My pearl necklace was sold for Spanish refugees. Victims, flotsam, the injured, the weak – they were important. I wasn't. The children weren't. I had my ring. I took it to a municipal pawnshop. It is a place where you take things and they give you money. I wore dark glasses and turned up my coat collar, like a spy." He looked as though he understood that. "The man behind the counter said that I was a married woman and I needed my husband's written consent. I said the ring was mine. He said nothing could be mine, or something to that effect. Then he said he might have given me something for the gold in the band of the ring but the stones were worthless. He said this happened in the finest of families. Someone had pried the real stones out of their setting."

"Who did that?"

"A husband. Who else would? Someone's husband – mine, or my mother's, or my mother's mother's, when it comes to that."

"With a knife?" said Riri. He said, "The man might have been pretending. Maybe he took out the stones and put in glass."

"There wasn't time. And they were perfect imitations – the right shapes and sizes."

"He might have had glass stones all different sizes."

"The women in the family never wondered if men were lying," she said. "They never questioned being dispossessed. They were taught to think that lies were a joke on the liar. That was why they lost out. He gave me the price of the gold in the band, as a favor, and I left the ring there. I never went back."

He put the lid on the box of stamps, and it fitted; he removed it, put it back, and said, "What time do you turn on your TV?"

"Sometimes never. Why?"

"At home I have it from six o'clock."

THE OLD MAN CAME IN with a pink-and-white face, bearing about him a smell of cold and of snow. He put down his shopping bag and took things out – chocolate and bottles and newspapers. He said, "I had to go all the way to the station for the papers. There is only one shop open, and even then I had to go round to the back door."

"I warned you that today was Christmas," Irina said.

Mr. Aiken said to Riri, "When I was still a drinking man this was the best hour of the day. If I had a glass now, I could put ice in it. Then I might add water. Then if I had water I could add whiskey. I know it is all the wrong way around, but at least I've started with a glass."

"You had wine with your lunch and gin instead of tea and I believe you had straight gin before lunch," she said, gathering up the beads and coins and the turpentine and making the table Riri's domain again.

"Riri drank that," he said. It was so obviously a joke that she turned her head and put the basket down and covered her laugh with her fingers, as she had when she'd opened the door to him – oh, a long time ago now.

"I haven't a drop of anything left in the house," she said. That didn't matter, the old man said, for he had found what he needed. Riri watched and saw that when he lifted his glass his hand did not tremble at all. What his grandmother had said about that was true.

They had early supper and then Riri, after a courageous try at keeping awake, gave up even on television, and let her make his bed of scented sheets, deep pillows, a feather quilt. The two others sat for a long time at the table, with just one lamp, talking in low voices. She had a pile of notebooks from which she read aloud and sometimes she showed Mr. Aiken things. He could see them through the chinks in the bamboo screen. He watched the lamp shadows for a while and then it was as if the lamp had gone out and he slept deeply.

THE ROOM WAS FULL of mound shapes, as it had been that morning when he arrived. He had not heard them leave the room. His Christmas watch had hands that glowed in the dark. He put on his glasses. It was half past ten. His grandmother was being just a bit loud at the telephone; that was what had woken him up. He rose, put on his slippers, and stumbled out to the bathroom.

"Just answer yes or no," she was saying. "No, he can't. He has been asleep for an hour, two hours, at least.... Don't lie to me – I am bound to find the truth out. Was it a tumor? An extrauterine pregnancy?... Well, look.... Was she or was she not pregnant? What can you mean by 'not exactly'? If you don't know, who will?" She happened to turn her head, and saw him and said without a change of tone, "Your son is here, in his pajamas; he wants to say good night to you."

She gave up the telephone and immediately went away so that the child could talk privately. She heard him say, "I drank some kind of alcohol."

So that was the important part of the day: not the journey, not the necklace, not even the strange old guest with the comic accent. She could tell from the sound of the child's voice that he was smiling. She picked up his bathrobe, went back to the hall, and put it over his shoulders. He scarcely saw her: he was concentrated on the distant voice. He said, in a matter-of-fact way, "All right, goodbye," and hung up.

"What a lot of things you have pulled out of that knapsack," she said.

"It's a large one. My father had it for military service."

Now, why should that make him suddenly homesick when his father's voice had not? "You are good at looking after yourself," she said. "Independent. No one has to tell you what to do. Of course, your mother had sound training. Once when I was looking for a nurse for your mother and her sisters, a great peasant woman came to see me, wearing a black apron and black buttoned boots. I said, 'What can you teach children?' And she said, 'To be clean and polite.' Your grandfather said, 'Hire her,' and stamped out of the room."

His mother interested, his grandfather bored him. He had the Christian name of a dead old man.

"You will sleep well," his grandmother promised, pulling the feather quilt over him. "You will dream short dreams at first, and by morning they will be longer and longer. The last one of all just before you wake up will be like a film. You will wake up wondering where you are, and then you will hear Mr. Aiken. First he will go round shutting all the windows, then you will hear his bath. He will start the coffee in an electric machine that makes a noise like a door rattling. He will pull on his snow boots with a lot of cursing and swearing and go out to fetch our croissants and the morning papers. Do you know what day it will be? The day after Christmas." He was almost asleep. Next to his watch and his glasses on a table close to the couch was an Astérix book and Irina's Russian box with old stamps in it. "Have you decided you want the stamps?"

"The box. Not the stamps."

He had taken, by instinct, the only object she wanted to keep. "For a special reason?" she said. "Of course, the box is yours. I am only wondering."

"The cover fits," he said.

She knew that the next morning he would have been here forever and that at parting time, four days later, she would have to remind him that leaving was the other half of arriving. She smiled, knowing how sorry he would be to go and how soon he would leave her behind. "This time yesterday..." he might say, but no more than once. He was asleep. His mouth opened slightly and the hair on his forehead became dark and damp. A doubled-up arm looked uncomfortable but Irina did not interfere; his sunken mind, his unconscious movements, had to be independent, of her or anyone, particularly of her. She did not love him more or less than any of her grandchildren. You see, it all worked out, she was telling him. You, and your mother, and the children being so worried, and my old friend. Anything can be settled for a few days at a time, though not for longer. She put out the light, for which his body was grateful. His mind, at that moment, in a sunny icicle brightness, was not only skiing but flying.

[1979]

BIOGRAPHICAL NOTES

ALICE ADAMS is the author of several collections of short stories and novels; most recently, *Superior Women* (Alfred A. Knopf, 1984), *Listening to Billy* (Viking Penguin, 1984) and *Families and Survivors* (Viking Penguin, 1984). She lives in San Francisco.

ANN BEATTIE is the author of short stories and novels; her most recent work is *Love Always* (Random House, 1985). She lives in Virginia.

JANE BOWLES's story was transformed from an unpublished manuscript fragment into its present form by Millicent Dillon and Paul Bowles. Her life is chronicled in *A Little Original Sin: The Life and Work of Jane Bowles* by Millicent Dillon (Holt, Rinehart & Winston, 1981). In 1978 Ecco Press issued *My Sister's Hand in Mine: An Expanded Edition of the Collected Works of Jane Bowles.*

LAURIE COLWIN's most recent works are *Passion and Affect* (Penguin Books, 1984) and *Shine On, Bright and Dangerous Object* (Penguin Books, 1984).

LOUISE ERDRICH's novel, *Love Medicine* (Holt, Rinehart & Winston, 1984) won the 1984 National Book Critics Circle Award.

TESS GALLAGHER is the author of three collections of poetry, most recently, *Willingly* (Graywolf Press, 1984). She teaches at Syracuse University.

MAVIS GALLANT, whose stories appear frequently in *The New Yorker*, is the author of *Home Truths* (Alfred A. Knopf, 1985). In 1984 Graywolf Press reissued her collection of stories, *Pegnitz Junction*.

BOBBIE ANN MASON won the 1982 Hemingway Foundation Award for her collection of short stories, *Shiloh and Other Stories*. Her first novel, *In Country*, has just been published by Harper & Row.

SUSAN MINOT's first collection of short stories is forthcoming from E. P. Dutton. She is Associate Editor at *Grand Street*.

ALICE MUNRO is the author of *The Beggar Maid: Stories of Flo and Rose* (Viking Penguin, 1984) and *The Moons of Jupiter* (Viking Penguin, 1984).

ELIZABETH TALLENT's first novel, *Museum Pieces*, was published by Alfred A. Knopf in 1985. Knopf also published *In Constant Flight*, a collection of short stories in 1983. She lives in New Mexico.

SARA VOGAN's novel *In Shelly's Leg* was recently issued in its first paperback edition by Graywolf Press. She lives and teaches in San Francisco.

JOY WILLIAMS's first collection of short stories, *Taking Care*, was published by Random House in 1982.